TRAFALGAR

James Grant,
HMS Norseman 1799–1806

by Bryan Perrett

SCHOLASTIC

While the events described and some of the characters in this book may be based on actual historical events and real people, James Grant is a fictional character, created by the author, and his story is a work of fiction.

Scholastic Children's Books
Commonwealth House, 1–19 New Oxford Street,
London, WC1A 1NU, UK
A division of Scholastic Ltd
London ~ New York ~ Toronto ~ Sydney ~ Auckland
Mexico City ~ New Delhi ~ Hong Kong

Published in the UK by Scholastic Ltd, 2002

Copyright © Bryan Perrett, 2002

ISBN 0 439 99421 7

All rights reserved
Typeset by TW Typesetting, Midsomer Norton, Somerset
Printed and bound in Great Britain by Mackays of Chatham Limited, Chatham, Kent
Midshipman John Russell (1811-1843) by Gordon John Watson. © NATIONAL
MARITIME MUSEUM, LONDON
Battle of Trafalgar 21st October 1805 by Thomas Whitcombe 1760-1824
Christies Images/Bridgeman Art Library

2 4 6 8 10 9 7 5 3 1

Liverpool, 1806

My name is James Grant and I was born twenty years ago in Liverpool where my father had established himself successfully as a merchant. My brother Alexander is ten years older than me and has now joined my father in the business. I also have two older sisters, Ailsa and Catriona, the former of whom is now married while the latter is still taking her pick of the young gentlemen who regularly call upon her. We live in Bold Street, which was on the outskirts of the town when it was built, but so rapid is Liverpool's expansion that soon there will be many dwellings beyond ours.

Over the last seven years, I have been at sea aboard His Majesty's frigate *Norseman*. The story which I am going to tell you, my story, is as faithful an account as I can muster, being based on my sea journal, plus numerous letters written at the time. I begin with my earliest memories of life among the docks of Liverpool...

1799

We were at war with France. Ever since I was very small the sight of French prisoners being brought ashore, mainly seamen from captured warships, had been a constant one. In 1799, the year I turned thirteen, they began to arrive ashore in increasing numbers, to be housed in the New Prison behind the Fort. For the most part, they seemed harmless enough, anxious to earn a shilling or two by selling model ships they had painstakingly carved from bone and other materials.

The present war began shortly after the Revolution in that country. Father said that the people were so ill-used and cruelly taxed that a revolution was bound to happen. He said, however, that it brought to power some of the most cruel, ruthless men who have ever walked the face of this earth. Not content with murdering their own King and Queen, as well as thousands of innocent folk, they would like the mob here to rise and do likewise, and have sent their agents to encourage them. War between us could not have been avoided if we were to preserve our freedom and law and order. Although the town itself was secure from attack, Liverpool ships were lost to French privateers. In return, we sent out our own privateers (which are private vessels equipped for war under a licence called Letters of Marque), to prey upon the enemy's commerce. Father said that the rewards could be enormous, but the risks were just as great.

Visits by any of the King's ships to the River Mersey were by no means welcome to everyone, as I discovered when walking one day with my mother along Dale Street, where numerous inns and taverns could be found. At first we were startled by the sight of men running, then there was a commotion as a naval party under a Lieutenant dragged several more out of an alehouse, a number of the latter bleeding from blows to the head. Mother said that it was the Press Gang, sent ashore to gather up men so that the ship's crew could be brought up to strength. They were after seamen, but they would sometimes take landsmen, labourers for preference, because they would be useful when it came to manning the heavy guns. By the time we had reached the alehouse, one or two seamen had been released after showing the officer their prized exemption certificates, but the Press Gang, brandishing their cudgels, had rounded up the rest of the party into a tight little knot. Pointing to a man with blood streaming down his face, Mother asked the Lieutenant why he had been treated so harshly. Touching his hat, the officer replied that the man had no proof of exemption and, contrary to the law of the land, had tried to resist the King's Press and had simply been restrained. He explained that unless the Royal Navy kept its ships fully manned it would be impossible to keep control of the sea, and that if this was lost the French would soon invade us. Mother said that she understood, but thought it a pity that men should be separated from their families in this way, perhaps for years if not for ever. The officer replied that he was not unsympathetic, but the world had become a dangerous place and we must use all the means at our disposal to keep the country safe.

One of my most vivid memories is when, as a small boy, I was taken to the Goree, a large warehouse on the waterfront, where my father had business with a

Mr Thomas Tarleton. We were told that Mr Tarleton was not in his counting house, but could be found in the vaults below. There he was conversing with a man whom I took to be an officer in the Army, who was accompanied by several soldiers, and a hard-looking countryman.

"Ah, Grant," said Mr Tarleton, catching sight of us. "Let me present Bandmaster Wilton of the Queen's Fusiliers, and also Mr Jake Barnton, steward to Lady Harmbury. Gentlemen, this is Mr Hamish Grant, one of the town's most respected merchants, and his son James."

"Your servant, Sir," said the two men, bowing.

Father replied as courteously, saying that he hoped we were not interrupting their business. At that moment an iron door at the end of the vault was opened and several manacled negroes were pushed into the room by Mr Tarleton's men. I had seen pictures of negroes before, but these were the first I had set eyes upon, so I remember the occasion well. There were four big fellows, and a little boy and girl. The men were dressed in white canvas shirts and trousers and the girl in a sort of shift. They rolled their eyes at us and seemed very frightened. Bandmaster Wilton prodded the men here and there, then pulled open their mouths to examine their teeth.

"They seem healthy enough," he commented. "Do they speak English?"

"They are indeed excellent specimens," replied Mr Tarleton's clerk. "Furthermore, having been born in the West Indies, English is their natural language, Sir."

"Glad to hear it," said Wilton. "I'll turn 'em into fine bandsmen who'll be a credit to the Regiment."

He then signed a paper and ordered his file of soldiers to lead the men out. The little boy and girl were now huddled together, crying.

"And what is to become of these two poor mites?" Father asked. I could see that he was becoming angry.

"The girl will become one of Her Ladyship's maids, and the boy will become a page, dressed as a Blackamoor," said Barnton, handing over a purse of coins to Tarleton's clerk. "Together, they will accompany Her Ladyship to all the fashionable events in London and Bath, for at the highest levels of society servants of this kind are now considered essential."

He bowed briefly and left, pushing the children roughly ahead of him up the stairs. Father turned immediately to Tarleton.

"This trafficking in human beings is utterly evil, Sir," he said, furiously. "It is high time the Government put an end to this infamous African Trade."

"I am, of course, aware of your views, Mr Grant," replied Tarleton, with a sneering sort of smile. "My opinion is that we do these people a service by rescuing them from their African savagery and transporting them to the Indies, where they perform useful work and learn the values of a Christian society. Besides, the slaves you have just seen will have a much better life than those they had left behind, cutting sugar cane in the fields."

"We shall agree to differ on that," said Father. They then concluded their business coldly and we left.

On the way home I asked Father what sort of business was the African Trade? He said that the West Indies, which produced sugar, molasses, spices, coffee and cotton, were so hot and disease-ridden that few Europeans could expect to survive for long there. Instead, large numbers of African slaves were being shipped to the Indies and the Americas to work on the plantations. Specially constructed ships, sometimes known as Blackbirders, would leave Liverpool and other ports loaded with cheap goods such as beads, knives, mirrors and brass bedsteads, bound for West Africa, where the cargo would be sold. The money was used to pay the African or Arab slave-catchers, who would hand over the slaves to be shipped across the Atlantic in conditions so terrible that many died. The slaves were then sold to the plantation owners, and the ship took on a valuable cargo of local produce that would be sold when she reached her home port. Each leg of the voyage, which was known as The Triple Passage, made a profit. Some Liverpool merchants, like Mr Tarleton, were deeply involved in the trade, and as the net profit from the sale of slaves alone amounted to well over £200,000 each year they naturally wanted it to continue. Father said that others, like himself, were determined that it should be stopped, and he believed that in the end they would win. I hoped he was right, because I was sorry for the slaves I had seen, who had hurt no one and did not deserve to be treated in this way.

❀ ☸ ❀

Shortly after my thirteenth birthday, Father asked me what thoughts I had regarding the life I was to lead. I was surprised, as I had not really thought about the future much, and said so.

"Well, would you like to join me and your brother Alexander in the business?" he asked.

I thought of our counting house where everyone seemed to be squabbling about a penny on this or a ha'penny off that, and of our ancient Chief Clerk,

Mr Cobbold, who after years of service had become so dry I thought you could blow the dust off him.

"I don't think so, Sir," I replied. "I hope you will not be disappointed, but I think I should find it very dull and be of little use to you."

"Nevertheless, James, we must consider some respectable profession which will enable you to support yourself," he said. "Would you, in due course, consider studying to become a minister of religion, or perhaps a physician, or even a lawyer?"

At school I had many friends, but I did not enjoy the work and the thought of spending more years learning from books was even worse than that of working in the counting house.

"I am sorry, Father, but I do not think so," I replied. "As you know, study does not come easily to me. I should really prefer a more active life."

"In that case," he said, "your choice is somewhat limited. If you wish to become a soldier, I cannot afford to buy a commission for you in the cavalry or the infantry. On the other hand, if you wish to become an artilleryman or an engineer you could be entered upon the books of the Royal Military Academy at Woolwich and thereby obtain the King's commission without the need to purchase."

This was something I had not considered, and it sounded attractive. On the other hand, whenever I had visited the waterfront with my Father I had listened to the seamen's tales of the faraway places they had been and the strange sights they had seen, and had told myself that one day I would visit these places and see for myself.

"I should really prefer to go to sea, Father," I said, at which he became thoughtful.

"It would be a simple matter for me to obtain an apprenticeship for you with one of the merchant captains of my acquaintance," he said at length. "However, that would place you in some danger not only from the French, but also of being taken off by a King's ship at sea to make up its crew. In such circumstances you would be employed as a common seaman, perhaps for years."

I knew this was true, for I had often heard merchant captains complaining that they had been left short-handed when warships had compulsorily recruited some of their crew.

"That being the case," Father continued, "it would be better to take the bull by the horns. Your mother has a distant younger cousin, Charlotte Montague, who has recently written to her saying that her husband has just been given command of a captured French frigate, presently undergoing an extensive refit at Portsmouth Dockyard. I shall enclose a note with her reply, asking whether a suitable arrangement can be made for you."

I replied that I should like that, inspired by the idea that perhaps one day I should serve under the famous Admiral Nelson, who in 1798 had destroyed an entire French fleet at the Battle of the Nile, leaving the army of General Bonaparte completely stranded in Egypt. Three weeks after our conversation I was surprised to receive a personal letter in the mails.

James Grant, Esq,
Bold Street,
Liverpool

My Dear Sir,
I have pleasure in advising you that I am authorized to offer you the appointment of Midshipman aboard HM Frigate Norseman, *presently refitting here at Portsmouth. Formal notification of this will follow through the official process. You will, I suspect, require a little time to put your affairs in order, but I suggest that you join me not later than 20th January. My*

clerk is enclosing a list of those necessary items that you should bring with you. I look forward to making your acquaintance and remain, Sir,

> *Yr ob't svnt,*
> *Charles Montague,*
> *Captain, Royal Navy*

Aboard HMS Norseman,
Portsmouth, 10th December 1799

The list was long and included a sea chest, two uniforms, two pairs of regulation shoes, changes of body linen, foul weather clothing, toiletries, towels, a regulation dirk (which is a sort of dagger), a telescope, a watch, a sextant for measuring the angle of the sun at noon, dividers and other navigational instruments, writing materials and much else besides. There followed, save for the celebration of Christmas, weeks of hustle and bustle as we got everything together. I attended the tailor several times and confess that I was not at first pleased with the fit of my uniforms, which seemed a little overlarge. The tailor, however, pointed out that I had plenty of growing to do yet and had allowed for that, saying that there was no point in spending my money on new uniforms before they were needed. After all, he said, a Midshipman's pay of £2 or so a month was not a fortune and might be needed for other things.

As the time approached for me to leave I began to have some doubts about the wisdom of my choice. Everyone said that life at sea was hard, and I was very comfortable at home. There was also the thought that I might not see my family again for years. I felt, however, that there could be no turning back, for I should be shamed in front of my friends if I changed my mind for these reasons.

Shortly after the New Year, Father and I visited the coaching office. They told us that as there was no direct service to Portsmouth, I should have to change coaches in London, from whence there were frequent departures. It was possible to travel to London on the Mail Coach, but Father advised against this as, while it takes but 37 hours, the journey was non-stop and an ordeal. I decided to book an inside seat on a slower coach which, while taking two-and-a-half days at that time of year, did stop overnight at inns, permitting the passengers some rest.

The packing of my sea chest was complete. Mother had included all manner of things that she hoped would please me, including jars of preserved meat and pickles, a bottle of brandy and an expensive caddy of tea. I also put in my flute, which I played tolerably well. The chest was now so heavy it was too much for me to lift. Father said one of his men would take it on a barrow to the coaching office, and that when I changed in London there were always idlers hanging around who would carry it for a few coins. On the side of the chest was painted MIDSHIPMAN JAMES GRANT – HMS NORSEMAN, so that there would be no doubt whose property it was.

January – February, 1800

On 10th January I was up betimes to catch the coach, my chest being stowed securely on the roof. For a moment, I felt a chill of apprehension because I was heading into an unknown world in which I knew no one and, as yet, had no friends. Then I told myself that I would discover so much that was new to me and meet many interesting people. So, it was with mixed feelings that I leaned out of the window to wave to my family as the guard sounded his horn and the coach clattered out into Dale Street. Having travelled inland as far as Warrington, we turned south through Cheshire and made steady progress, halting from time to time to change horses. This was always speedily done, the fresh teams always being ready and harnessed at the staging posts to await our arrival. Sometimes, where the Turnpike companies had made a good road, we bowled along, but in other places the roads were sometimes no better than rutted tracks and we had to proceed more slowly. As my thoughts were fully occupied with the future, I did not notice my fellow passengers much. We stopped the first night at Stafford, where the driver and guard joined me while we dined on beef, boiled onions and potatoes, washed down with ale. They were to take a coach back to Liverpool the next day and said we had been lucky because the previous night's severe frost had hardened the road. People did not travel at this time of year unless they had to, the driver told me. There were times, he said, when coaches could be marooned in deep snow, and on one occasion an outside passenger had frozen to death, so bitter was the cold.

Setting off at dawn next day with a new driver and guard, we reached Rugby by nightfall, where we dined on lamb cutlets and vegetables. The accommodation was clean and comfortable. Never having been outside Liverpool before, I received many surprises, the first of which was the number of different accents I encountered. Father, of course, is a Scot and he has a Scottish accent. Again, the many Irishmen and Welshmen in Liverpool have their own accents, but I expected that as Scotland, Ireland and Wales are different countries. What surprised me was that people in different parts of England should also have their own accents.

We set off with a new driver and guard before it was fully light, but now we were travelling along the route of an old Roman road called Watling Street, and as it was well maintained we made excellent progress, reaching London early the same afternoon. I had my chest taken to the premises of the Portsmouth coach company and reserved a seat for the morning of the 15th. I then took a room for two nights in an inn recommended by the coach company and decided to spend the next day exploring the capital.

I reached Portsmouth shortly after nightfall on the 15th. Not knowing my way about, I again spent the night at an inn. Next morning I walked round the harbour until I discovered where *Norseman* was lying. She was handsome but higher in the water than I expected, so that her copper bottom was showing. Having constantly accompanied my father along the waterfront at home, I knew a little about the construction of ships and her foremast seemed to be absent, and while the main and mizzen masts were standing with their yards in place, the latter seemed to be bare of canvas. It felt a little strange that she was to become my new home.

I returned to the inn and arranged for a man to trundle my chest down to the nearest landing steps, where I waited. At length a boat pulled away from the ship's side and reached the steps. As a worried-looking Lieutenant stepped out I raised my hat to him and asked whether he was from the *Norseman*. Returning the compliment, he said he was and enquired the nature of my business. I gave him my name and told him I had orders to report aboard. He introduced himself as Emerson, the ship's Second Lieutenant, and said that he had business in the dockyard that was likely to take several hours, so he would have me taken out. Two of the seamen heaved my chest into the boat. As I sat down on one of the rowers' seats, which are called thwarts, the crew began grinning but made no further move.

"You're new to the Navy, aren't you, Sir?" said a big seaman I took to be the leading hand.

"Yes, this is my first day," I replied. "I have never been to sea before."

"Ah, then, you won't know," he continued. "Being an officer, you sits in the stern of a boat – otherwise we can't shove off."

Feeling rather foolish, I thanked him and moved to the seat in the stern. The boat shoved off and in steady strokes we pulled across the harbour. The *Norseman* loomed ever larger until, as we came alongside, she seemed to tower over us.

"Officer aboard!" shouted the leading hand. "Up you go, Sir!" he said, indicating some steps on the side of the hull leading to a break in the bulwarks called the entry port.

I climbed to the deck, raising my hat to the Quarter Deck and the Officer of the Watch as Father said I should.

"Dacres, First Lieutenant," said the officer. "Who might you be?"

"James Grant, Midshipman, Sir, reporting aboard as ordered," I replied, handing him my papers.

"Are you, now?" he said, eyeing me sharply. He did not seem to be a man who encouraged conversation. At length, he turned to a seaman nearby.

"Boatswain's Mate, take Mr Midshipman Grant below and see that his chest follows. Then give the Gunner my compliments and ask him to get the officer snugged down."

"Aye aye, Sir!"

The Boatswain's Mate, a burly man in a check shirt and a black, wide-brimmed hat, took me to the lower deck in the after part of the vessel. I looked towards the stern and saw a line of cabin doors on either side. In between was a polished table and chairs. It all looked very comfortable and, having been aboard merchant vessels with Father, was what I had expected. A middle-aged man in a blue jacket and brass buttons arrived. He introduced himself as Mr Short, the Gunner, and said he was responsible for the Midshipmen. I asked him which cabin was mine. He guffawed.

"You don't have a cabin, Mr Grant!" he said, chuckling. "Midshipmen aren't part of the Gunroom mess. That's for the ship's Lieutenants and Senior Warrant Officers, so don't you ever set foot in there until you're asked!"

He pointed to a partitioned area nearby, little larger than a theatre box, enclosing a scrubbed table and two benches.

"That's the Midshipmen's berth, and you sling your hammock from those hooks in the deckhead."

Once again, I had made a fool of myself and, feeling awkward, thought it best to admit my ignorance.

"I'm afraid I know nothing at all about the Navy, Mr Short," I said. "It seems as though I've an awful lot to learn."

"That you have, Mr Grant," he said, not unkindly. "That you have. But we've all of us had to start somewhere, at some time or other, so people will make allowances."

He went through the contents of my chest, saying he regretted the necessity of doing so, but some young gentlemen were so keen to be at the French that they brought pistols aboard with them, making them a danger to themselves and everyone else. He said I seemed well provided for, then put aside the various additional items Mother had included, saying that unless I had any objection it would be wise to conform with the custom of the Midshipmen's mess, where such things were shared by all. On my saying that I had no objection, he summoned the Midshipmen's steward, a small swarthy man called Pedro, telling him to put the items in his pantry, then find Mr Midshipman Shipley and ask him to join us.

"You and I will be seeing a lot more of each other," said the Gunner, turning to me. "For the moment, though, I've much to attend to, so I'll leave it to Mr Shipley to help you settle in and find your way around."

Gerard Shipley was a friendly sort, but much older than I had expected. He said he was aged 22 and therefore old for a Midshipman. He was, he explained, unable to pass the Examination for Lieutenant, for although he knew the theory and was well versed in practical details, having been at sea for eight years, he simply went to pieces when confronted by an Examining Board of glowering Captains. He took me to the Purser's store to draw hammocks, of which I am entitled to two, but I had to buy my own stuffed mattress and blankets. Gerard showed me how to hang my hammock, make a bed and climb into it – which was no easy matter – then take it down, roll it and lash it neatly until it resembled a sort of sausage.

After I had practised this for an hour or so it was time for dinner and I met the other occupants of the Midshipmen's berth, who were all my own age or a year or two older. In all, *Norseman* had six Midshipmen: Keith Butler was the son of a naval officer; Jem Ainsworth was of prosperous farming stock and played the fiddle; Peter Dunn, who said what he liked least about the Navy was the lack of opportunity to play cricket, came from a family of bankers in the City of London; Octavius Merredew was the eighth son of a clergyman. Dinner consisted of dumpling stew, bread, cheese and a small beer. I could not but notice that some of the others picked on Octavius, who stuttered and fumbled and was of small and puny frame. They hid his cutlery, and when he found it he discovered that his plate had vanished. He regularly received slaps across the back of his head.

After dinner, Jem and I played a tune or two, listened to with interest by the seamen at nearby tables. I then wrote a note to my parents and turned in. So ended my first day in the Royal Navy. Everything was so strange and different from the world I was used to that I was unsure whether I should like the life or not.

The day began before it was light. I found my hammock to be unexpectedly comfortable, though I was once painfully pitched out on to the deck when turning over. At six o'clock I was awakened by a Petty Officer's shouts of "Lash up and stow!" The seamen tumbled out of their hammocks, and having lashed them into the sausage shape I had been shown, headed for the upper deck with them. We did likewise, although I botched my first attempt at lashing and had to do it again. Gerard then took me to the upper deck and told me to deposit my hammock, along with the others, in some netting that ran along the top of the bulwarks. He said that it not only kept them out of the way, but would also provide some protection against the enemy's musketry fire when we were in action. After washing we breakfasted upon lumpy porridge, bread, preserves and coffee.

On deck groups of seamen were hard at work laying out what seemed to be miles of rope under the direction of the Boatswain. I saw a strange-looking craft set off from the dockyard towards us, propelled slowly by long oars that made her look like a giant beetle. She seemed to be fitted with a framework of long timbers that some of her crew were hauling into an upright position.

"What sort of craft is that?" I asked Gerard.

"She's called a shear hulk and is bringing us out our new foremast," he explained. "Once alongside, she will hoist the lower mast into place. Once it has been secured, shrouds will be rigged and a working platform known as a top constructed. Likewise, the topmast will be hoisted aboard and joined to the lower mast by two wooden caps that join both. The topmast will then be joined to the topgallant mast. The yards can then be hoisted into place and secured. The process of re-rigging can then begin in earnest, starting forward and working back along the ship."

At this point a shout came from the quarterdeck:

"Mr Midshipman Grant – lay aft!"

"That means you're to report to the senior officer on the quarterdeck," said Gerard. "Better be quick about it – they don't like to be kept waiting!"

I was met by Mr Dacres, the First Lieutenant, who eyed me much as he would an insect.

"Your uniform fits you but ill," he said. "Was it made for a larger man?"

"No, Sir," I replied. "It was made large so that I should grow into it."

"Indeed, Sir," he said. "Then either you had better grow considerably or it had better shrink during the next 24 hours, or you and I will cease to be good friends. Find the ship's tailor and have something done about it. Now, the Captain wishes to see you. Speak when you are spoken to, and not before."

He took me down to the Captain's cabin, where a firm voice bade us enter in answer to a knock. From the tone of his letter I had expected Captain Montague to be a friendly individual, but such was not the case. He was standing with his clerk at the table in the stern cabin, surrounded by official papers. In contrast to Mr Dacres, who was tall, fair-haired and seemed to wear a permanent scowl, the Captain was of average height and of grim appearance. There was, too, a hint of bitter humour about his face, and his eyes bored into mine until I felt he could read my innermost thoughts.

"Mr Midshipman Grant, Sir," said Dacres.

"Ah, yes, the last of our Midshipmen," said the Captain. "You'll oblige me by conveying my compliments to your parents when next you write, Mr Grant."

I said that I would.

"You join us at a most fortunate time," he continued. "During the next few weeks you will work as you have never worked before. You will discover muscles you never knew existed, you will become dirty, wet, cold and very tired, and you will probably wonder why you ever bothered to join us. At the end of it, you will have learned all there is to know about running and standing rigging, and the name of every sail we carry. Is that not a worthwhile endeavour?"

I said that it was, and asked whether we would be serving under Admiral Nelson. A hint of a smile appeared at the corners of the Captain's mouth.

"For the moment, I rather doubt it, Mr Grant. Once we have refitted and I am satisfied that we have a good fighting ship and crew, we shall be escorting a convoy of merchantmen to the West Indies, which your father will have told you are of enormous economic value to us. The Indies will remain our permanent station, so you will be away from home for some years to come. However, in that time all things are possible and Admiral Nelson may yet have the pleasure of making your acquaintance."

He turned to the First Lieutenant, his expression suddenly businesslike.

"It will encourage the hands to have the Midshipmen working among them, Mr Dacres. See to it that the Gunner has our young gentlemen suitably dressed from the slop chest, if you please. Tar and uniforms do not mix well together. Thank you, gentlemen, that is all."

Mindful of Mr Dacres' criticism, on leaving the cabin I immediately sought out the ship's tailor with my spare uniform coat. I explained my predicament to him but he was not sympathetic until I offered to pay him for his work. He then brightened somewhat, saying that he thought he could take in sufficient of the slack yet retain enough cloth to allow for my growth. The £10 I was given on leaving home had now shrunk considerably.

I returned to the Midshipmen's berth to find the Gunner handing out old shirts and trousers from the slop chest. He said these would be needed next day for the heavy work we were to undertake, but in the meanwhile Mr Shipley could spend the rest of the day showing me round the ship so that I could get my bearings properly.

Gerard said that in French hands the ship had been named *Normandie*, but as that wasn't acceptable to the

Admiralty she was now called *Norseman*. She had been knocked about a bit when captured, hence the need for a complete refit. Officially, she was now a Sixth Rate armed with 28 guns, although like most ships she carried rather more. In fact she carried twenty-four 18-pounder guns on the upper deck, four 24-pounder carronades and two 6-pounder stern chasers on the quarterdeck, and two 24-pounder carronades and two 6-pounder bow chasers on the forecastle.

"What is a carronade?" I asked Gerard.

"That is," he said, pointing to a short, stubby gun mounted on a slide. "It's a fearful weapon at close range, throwing a heavy ball that will cause immense damage to an enemy's hull. We call the carronades our Smashers."

Seamen were busy all over the ship, especially around the new foremast. I could barely understand what the seaman and petty officers were saying, being unable as yet to distinguish between nautical terms and a type of cursing that I had never heard before. Gerard laughed and said I would soon learn. To avoid getting in the way of those working forward, we went below and passed through the seamen's quarters. Their clothing was stowed in bags that hung from pegs in the side of the hull. Their plates, bowls and mugs were kept in racks alongside. They sat on chests or boxes around ingeniously constructed tables that could be hinged upwards to lie against the racks when they were not required for meals. Each seaman was allowed eighteen inches of space in which to sling his hammock.

"At the moment there's plenty of room for everyone," said Gerard. "We've only got half the men aboard we need to bring us up to our authorized complement of 200. When the rest start arriving it will begin to seem cramped."

"Where will they come from?" I asked.

"Well, there'll be a detachment of Marines, of course, and a few volunteers who enlisted for the bounty payment they'll receive," he replied. "The rest will be men from the prisoner-of-war hulks who agreed to serve in exchange for their freedom, whoever the press gang could bring in and, no doubt, the usual crowd of jail sweepings."

I remembered the encounter my mother and I had once had with the press gang in Liverpool. Their victims had at least been honest men, but Gerard's reference to jail sweepings alarmed me.

"D'you mean convicts?" I asked.

"Yes, but of the lesser kind. Petty thieves, habitual

drunkards, brawlers and such who've been sentenced to a term of imprisonment or transportation to Australia for a number of years. By volunteering for service in the Royal Navy they escape their sentences. Most of them will be knocked into shape, but there are always a few who will never change their ways, whatever punishment they receive."

We looked into the galley, where the cooks were hard at work. Their stove and oven rested on a brick hearth and had a metal chimney that passed through the deck above. The fire was enclosed and could not be left unattended, for fire at sea is a terrible thing. Next we went to the magazine, where the gunpowder is stored but which was empty for the moment. Gerard commented that this was another area of potential danger. In action two wet canvas curtains covered the entrance, through which charges were passed to the powder monkeys, who ran with them to the guns. Those within the magazine wore felt slippers to reduce the chance of striking a spark on loose grains of powder, working by the dark light of a horn lantern. Horn was used because it would not break if the lantern fell, whereas the glass in a normal lantern would, exposing the flame.

"Needless to say," Gerard commented, "if there was

an explosion down here the ship would be blown apart and most of us with her."

I was then shown in turn the shot lockers which held the balls for the cannons and the carronades, the various storerooms belonging to the Gunner, the Boatswain and the Carpenter, the sail rooms, again empty for the present, the cable tier, in which the anchor cable was stowed when the anchor was raised, and the hold, which contained the dry provisions store, the bread room, beef barrels and fresh water casks.

"The water will be well laced with lime juice," said Gerard. "It seems to prevent scurvy breaking out among the crew."

Seeing a door heavily bolted and barred, I asked him what lay within. He told me that it was used for storing rum, of which the seamen received a daily ration called grog, and which had to be kept beyond the reach of temptation. Returning to the deck, he showed me the bilge water pumps and finally the ship's wheel, describing the system of ropes and pulleys that worked upon the tiller below and so altered the position of the rudder.

I had learned a great deal and was amazed that so much could be compressed within so small a space.

When I settled down to dinner that evening I no longer felt quite as strange as I did when I first came aboard. The Gunner entered our berth, telling us that on the morrow we should dress in our slop-chest clothes and the names of the Boatswain's Mates we should each report to for our part in rigging the ship.

As the Captain had promised, during the days that followed I worked harder than I had ever done in my life. Gradually, however, the ship's rigging ceased to be the tangled mystery to me it once was. We began on the standing rigging for the foremast, including backstays, forestays, shrouds and ratlines, then progressed to the stays between the foremast and the bowsprit and the main- and foremast. The ropes forming the standing rigging had been soaked in tar, so that our hands, clothes and hair were covered in the stuff and we smelt strongly of it. Now I finally understood why seamen were called Jack Tars. Next, the yards were hoisted into place on the foremast and secured, a skilled task for which we were only required to provide the muscle to haul them aloft. Then came the running rigging, which, being less tar-soaked, was easier to handle.

Once the rigging was complete, a barge came alongside with many spare sails from the sailmakers' loft in the dockyard. One suit was stored below and the other we began to fit at once. The main and foremast each had a mainsail, a topsail and a topgallant sail which hung from the yards, while the mizzen had a topsail and a topgallant sail. These are all known as square sails. They are hoisted aloft to the level of the yards, to which they are secured by ropes passing through eyes in the top of the sail then tied over the top of the yard. To do this, one has to make one's way out along the yard, using the foot ropes rigged beneath. At first I found this very frightening. The deck seemed far below, even from the mainyard, and the water even further, but I watched what the seamen were doing and copied them, so that in the end I managed it without too much trouble.

The sailors seemed to enjoy our working among them as it gave them a chance to show off their own skills and point out our numerous mistakes. The Boatswain had attached an able seaman to each of us – save Gerard, who had done this many times before – partly to show us what was required and partly to see that we didn't get ourselves into trouble. I was lucky in that my instructor was Richard Corbett, the big man in the boat that first brought me out to the ship. Before we were first sent aloft he gave me some sound advice.

"You may wonder, Mr Grant, why the Good Lord has given you two hands," he said. "Well, he's given you one to look after yourself while you're up there, and the other belongs to the ship. Remember, think what you're about to do, don't move unless it's safe to do so, keep your feet spread on the foot ropes and decide what's within a hand's reach to steady yourself if the need arises."

My confidence grew each time we went aloft. I learned to let the yard take my weight while I leaned over it to reef, that is take in newly hung sails, using the lines of short ropes stitched into both sides of the sail and tying them neatly over the furled canvas. Becoming overconfident as the days went by, I became careless and nearly fell, earning a reprimand from Corbett.

"Mr Grant, you got away with that because we're lying in still waters. At sea, the ship will pitch and roll, so you've got to think twice as hard about what you're about to do. Make a mistake like that again and you're a dead man, so don't you go saying you haven't been warned!"

I think I must have looked mortified as he continued, not unkindly, "Plain fact is, Mr Grant, if you fall you will either hit the deck or go overboard. If you hit the deck after falling from the topsail yard you will make a mess that we shall have to clear up before we commit your remains to the deep. If you go overboard it will take time to bring the ship to and launch a boat. Even then, a head is difficult to spot in any sort of sea. What's worse, in some parts the sea's so cold you'll have frozen to death before we can get to you, and in others it's so warm you could provide a tasty dinner for the sharks. So it's worth taking a bit of time and trouble about what you're doing now – am I right, Mr Grant?"

I said he was and thereafter curbed my enthusiasm. Octavius, however, had no such enthusiasm and was unable to conceal his fear of heights. Even while working on the mainyard he seemed paralysed and was sweating profusely. At length, his instructor, a tough, hard-faced man named Grigg, lost patience with him.

"You're supposed to be a junior officer, Mr Merredew, Sir!" he snarled. "What are we supposed to think when you can't do what the rest of us can?"

"I'm s-sorry," said Octavius, miserably. "I hate heights. They make me d-dizzy."

"Not good enough, Sir!" snapped Grigg. "You've got to get a grip of your fear and show it who's master. Get back to the maintop."

Gingerly, Octavius did as he was told, but if he thought he was going below he was mistaken. On reaching the platform, Grigg pointed upwards.

"Up the ratlines to the topsail yard, if you please, Mr Merredew," said Grigg. "I'll be right behind you."

Slowly, Octavius climbed the rope ladder until the yard was reached.

"Now," said Grigg, "out along the port foot ropes until you reach the end. Concentrate on what you're doing and don't look down."

"I c-can't," replied Octavius, helplessly. It seemed to me that he was close to tears.

"You can and you will, Sir, because we won't be going down until you've done it! Now, make a start!"

From below, I watched in horror. At first, Octavius seemed unable to move, then he stretched out a foot to the rope and took a grip over the yard. Then he moved the other foot on to the rope and edged his way along, leaning across the yard. Although Grigg was close behind him, I expected him to fall as he changed to the second foot rope, but he did not. He reached the third foot rope and, momentarily looking down as he felt for it, seemed to freeze. Then, with the courage of desperation, he took the last few steps and lay across the yard, apparently exhausted.

"There, Mr Merredew, you've faced up to it and you've won," I heard Grigg say to him. "It's no different up here than it is down on the mainyard, is it, Sir? Now, I'm going to tell you something that will please you. Apart from Mr Shipley, who's spent half his life in the Navy, for the moment there isn't a Midshipman aboard who has been as high as you have today. Come on, let's go down."

Octavius managed to grin and retraced his steps with greater confidence. The incident was referred to at dinner that night.

"Didn't I see you up on the main topsail yard this afternoon?" asked Keith Butler.

"What? Oh yes, that's right," Octavius replied airily, as though nothing important had happened. "When you're ready, they'll let you up there, I expect."

"You'll soon be swinging round the ropes like a chimpanzee!" said Jem Ainsworth.

"Ha! Ha! Just think of it – Monkey Merredew!" chortled Peter Dunn, jabbing his fork into Octavius' neck. Octavius promptly responded by punching Peter's nose so hard that it bled. Gerard broke up the fight before it got started. The Gunner had already warned us that he would have no fighting in the Midshipmen's berth, or those involved would kiss his daughter, by which he meant bending the offenders over a gun and giving their rumps twelve painful whacks each with his cane. After that, the others began treating Octavius in a more friendly way.

We worked so hard that days soon turned into weeks. While the rigging was taking place a constant procession of boats and barges was reaching the ship. They brought with them powder kegs, ammunition, small arms, fresh water casks, beef barrels, sacks of flour, cheese, vegetables and many other essential supplies, all of which had to be stowed when we were not working aloft.

The crew, too, had almost been brought up to strength by fresh arrivals. The volunteers seemed to be a mixed lot. Some of them had enlisted because of the bounty they had been offered, using the money to buy their way out of the debtors' prison, while others had sent it to their families, who were in dire need of it. Others, again, had their own private reasons for wishing to disappear from the land for a while – one was overjoyed that he had escaped from his nagging wife. Twenty-four scarlet-coated Marines, including a lieutenant, a sergeant, two corporals and a drummer, also came aboard. Gerard explained that the Marines always sling their hammocks between the officers and the seamen because part of their duties involves protecting the former against mutiny by the latter. This was in everyone's minds since the dreadful conditions under which seamen were forced to serve resulted in the 1797 mutinies in the fleets at Spithead and the Nore. The men's grievances were dealt with fairly then and I observed that our own crew, though given to grumbling constantly among themselves, showed no hostility towards the officers. A dozen men arrived from the prisoner-of-war hulks, including Danes, Dutchmen, two Americans and three Frenchmen who said they were Royalists at heart and hated the present government in Paris. They were all experienced seamen, taken from enemy ships of war. The press gang brought in another ten, four of whom were merchant seamen and the rest waterfront idlers. Some seemed resigned to their fate, while others were bewildered and depressed. Last of all came the jail sweepings, some fifteen in number, escorted aboard by a file of soldiers. They were either sullen and surly, or given to insolent smirks, or keen to gain the goodwill of any in authority. One of this group towered above the rest. His was a face to avoid on a dark night. His brows were lowering, his nose had been broken at least once and one of his ears was shapeless. When one of the soldiers tried to hurry him along with a shove, the man turned on him angrily.

"Take your hands off me or I'll tear you apart!" he snarled.

"Behave yourself!" yelled a Petty Officer, cutting the man sharply across the rump with a rope's end. "And you can stow that kind of gab for a start!"

Sullenly, the man followed the other criminals below. Captain Montague was said to be furious that the pressed men and convicts had been sent aboard before we were ready for sea, blaming the muddle on delays caused by the dockyard. He ordered that they should be confined to the forecastle under guard until we were clear of the land. Even so, the big man who had given us trouble earlier managed to escape through a gun port, although he was picked up by the guard boat as he tried to swim ashore. He was put in irons, that is, shackled to the deck, to await his punishment.

By evening the officers were all in the foulest of moods, caused by their dealings with the various dockyard officials, whom they accused variously of being corrupt, idle, incompetent, inefficient or mentally defective. I thought they exaggerated, but they snapped at each other and everyone who dared to cross their path, so it was best to make oneself scarce.

March, 1800

After a month on board *Norseman* I was told that as I write a fair hand, I was to assist the First Lieutenant while he prepared the watchkeeping bills. I was not pleased, as my experience so far had been that he was not the friendliest of men. When I reported to his cabin after breakfast he asked how I was getting on, but before I could reply he said he was pleased to hear it and told me to sit opposite him at his table. He was responsible to the Captain for the ship's discipline, administration and efficiency, so he was a very busy man and it is small wonder that he was sometimes short-tempered.

He first handed me the divisions list and told me to make two fair copies. The ship's crew was divided equally into divisions, each of which was commanded by a Lieutenant who was responsible for the health and welfare of the men within it. When I had finished I was given a list of stations to copy. This showed how the crew were distributed throughout the ship. There were the foretopmen, maintopmen and mizzentopmen, who are regarded as the best seamen aboard and who were experts at working aloft among the rigging. Then there were the forecastle men, the waisters stationed amidships, and the afterguard, whose responsibilities included the quarterdeck. Then came the Marines, the Boatswain's Mates, the Quartermasters, who were responsible for steering the ship, the Gunner's crew, the Carpenter's crew and finally the Idlers. The last were not really idle, but were men with their own specialized work to perform, such as the cooks, the sailmaker, the armourer, the cooper, officers' servants, the tailor and the shoemaker.

While I was thus engaged, the watchkeeping officers, including the Master and his Mates, were called in to comment on the draft watchkeeping bill that the First Lieutenant had prepared. Some said that they did not want such-and-such a man on their watch, others that they wanted a particular individual on theirs. The First Lieutenant made a number of alterations and handed the final draft for me to copy. All those who were not Idlers were assigned to two watches, the Larboard and the Starboard. The system was designed so that all the men had a reasonable time in which to rest and sleep, yet not perform the same watches each day. For example, the Larboard Watch took the First Watch from eight pm until midnight, slept until four am then took the Morning Watch until eight am, when hammocks were stowed and breakfast eaten. From nine am until noon, when dinner was taken, it was engaged upon drill, exercise or shipboard tasks. It remained at leisure until supper at four pm, then immediately took the First Dog Watch, lasting two hours. At eight pm it could hang its hammocks and turn in. The Starboard Watch alternated with the Larboard throughout the day and on the next the duties of the two watches were reversed.

The regulation of the watches was carried out by strokes on the ship's bell and was the responsibility of one of the watch's Quartermasters. He used two sand hourglasses, one of four hours' duration, this being the length of a watch, and the other of 30 minutes' duration. He struck the bell once 30 minutes after the watch had begun, twice 30 minutes later, and so on. Thus, eight bells signalled the end of a full watch, or four bells in the case of a Dog Watch.

My writing task kept me busy until late in the afternoon. During the day the First Lieutenant was summoned by the Captain. He returned to say that we would be sailing on the morning tide to relieve a frigate off the French coast, where she was blockading the enemy ships in harbour.

"We shan't be out there long," he added. "This will be more in the nature of a shakedown cruise before we leave for the Indies."

"Shakedown cruise, Sir?" I said, not understanding.

"Yes. We'll see how everyone shakes down together when they start working as a crew. Gives us a chance to iron out any problems. By the way, the Channel can be nasty at this time of year, so you'll need your foul-weather clothing. Now, hurry up and finish what you're doing!"

On the morning of 15th March both watches were required for leaving harbour. There were over 60 men, including the Marines, standing at the bars around the capstan, which provided the power for raising the anchor. When the signal was given the capstan party began heaving at their bars, which slowly began to move, hauling in the dripping anchor cable. One of the men struck up a shanty, singing one line, to which the entire party responded with the next.

King Louis was the King of France before the Revol-oo-tion,
Heave away boys, heave boys, heave!

And then he went and lost his head, it spoiled his
constit-oo-tion,
Heave away boys, heave boys, heave!

The pace increased until we could hear the steady tramp of the Marines' boots on the deck as their pace around the capstan became quicker. Suddenly the Boatswain, Mr McLeod, who had been leaning over the bows, held up his hand with a shout of, "Anchor's aweigh! Handsomely, now." The capstan party slowed down and finally halted at the command "Avast heaving!" Mr McLeod and his party then secured the anchor and lashed it into place. "All secure forrard, Sir!" shouted the Boatswain to the Quarterdeck.

Meanwhile, under the Captain's direction, the Master, Mr Rowcroft, was giving orders for making sail through his speaking trumpet. I was surprised that it was all done so quietly. All he said was, "Jib, Fore, Main and Mizzen Topsails and Spanker!" and the sails appeared like magic. *Norseman* was now alive and, as well as the excitement I felt at leaving harbour, I was proud to be aboard her.

We soon reached open water. The huge White Ensign flying from our gaff began to stream in the breeze, while the long commissioning pendant unfurled, reaching out into the sky from aloft. We must have made a grand sight. *Norseman* was now in her own element, rolling gently in the Channel swell while her bows rose and fell as they pushed through the waves, sometimes sending up a cloud of spray that sparkled in the sunlight. For all that it was bitterly cold I loved it, but those for whom the motion was too severe were already hanging over the rail to empty their stomachs. Telling Mr Dacres that the pressed men and criminals could be released, the Captain went below. An hour later there came an unexpected pipe accompanied by the cry from the Petty Officers, "Hands to witness punishment! All hands!"

The Midshipmen joined the officers on the Quarterdeck.

"What's happening?" I asked Gerard.

"It's the convict who tried to swim ashore," he replied. "The Captain's awarded him 36 lashes."

The Marines were drawn up below us, facing the seamen, who had assembled in the waist. The man was spread-eagled to a grating that had been lifted, tied to it securely by his wrists and ankles. His shirt had been removed, revealing an immensely strong physique marred by striped scars across his back. Two of the Boatswain's Mates were fastening a thick leather girdle around the man's kidneys, examining the scars as they did so.

"So you've been here before then?" I heard one of them comment.

"Aye, and it will take better men than you to break me!" said the prisoner defiantly, although he accepted a pad of leather pushed between his teeth.

The Captain stepped forward to the Quarterdeck rail, holding the open Punishment Book in his hand. A silence fell over the crew as he began to read:

"Ordinary Seaman Joel Armstrong, awarded 36 lashes for attempted desertion. Commence the punishment!"

"Start the roll!" ordered the Marine sergeant. The drummer began a long roll as the Boatswain's Mates took up their cat-o'-nine-tails.

"Lay on!" said the Boatswain, counting the strokes as each of them applied the lash in turn. "One ... two ... three ... four..."

I looked away after the fifth stroke, which drew blood.

"...thirty-four ... thirty-five ... thirty-six."

The drum roll stopped with a double tap and I looked up. The sight of the man's back, now a mass of flayed flesh, made me feel sick. A bucket of salt water was thrown on to it, the leather pad was removed from his mouth and he was untied. The surgeon examined him as he stood swaying, commenting that he would be fit for duty in a week. Throughout his ordeal, Armstrong had made not a sound, and even now there was the hint of an insolent smile as he glared up at the Captain. Some of the seamen were regarding him with open admiration.

"Now listen to what I have to say," said the Captain. "I run a tight ship because that is an efficient ship. No man who does his duty by the ship, his officers and his shipmates has anything to fear from me. Any man who fails in those duties now knows what to expect. Remember that. Mr Dacres, dismiss the ship's company, if you please."

Only Gerard had anything to say about the flogging over dinner, commenting that it was best such a lesson was taught early, then everyone knew where they stood. The French coast appeared shortly before sunset. It was just a smudge on the horizon.

We were continuously at sea until we were relieved by another frigate and then returned to Portsmouth harbour to replenish our stores. Having become used to keeping watches, I learned to value my sleep. There was a sameness about each day at sea, but there were times when gales forced us to withdraw from the

French coast to avoid being driven aground. I was perpetually cold and often wet, despite my good set of foul-weather oilskins. Whenever the weather improved the Captain ordered Beat to Quarters, which meant "prepare for action". Every officer and man then ran to his allotted station, mine being the Captain's messenger on the Quarterdeck. The partitions between cabins were dismantled, the decks were cleared and sanded, the guns were run in ready for loading and the netting rigged.

There were two types of netting. One, left intentionally slack, was intended to stop the enemy's boarders swarming aboard. Gerard said it was seldom used as it was usually shot to pieces in action. The other was called a *sauve-tête* and was slung taut over the open deck to prevent rigging, spars, blocks and so on, shot away by the enemy, from falling on those below. This seemed to me to be a very sensible precaution. The Captain never seemed to be satisfied with the time taken from the beating of Quarters until the First Lieutenant reported the ship ready for action. He made cutting comments to Mr Dacres, who reprimanded the other Lieutenants, who reprimanded the Petty Officers under their immediate command. In their turn, the Petty Officers lashed out with their ropes' ends to spur the men to greater speed the next time the ship cleared for action. The first attempt took eleven minutes, which was eventually reduced to six. But the Captain said he was still not satisfied.

When not practising going to Quarters, the crew exercised endlessly at the guns. I noticed that each member of the gun crew barely moved from the spot on which he stood, so that he would not get in the way of the neighbouring crew. They went through the motions of loading, using the rammer skilfully, running out the guns and aiming and firing. The Gunner, Mr Short, said that when, in reality, the guns were fired, their recoil itself ran them inboard ready for reloading. The chamber must then be sponged from the water tub beside each gun so that any residue of burning powder from the previous discharge was quenched before the next charge was loaded. Unless this was done there existed a real risk of a premature explosion resulting in death or injury among the gun crew. The carronades were easier to manage than the cannon as their recoil was contained by a specially designed slide and, being shorter, they required less space for loading. Mr Short drove the gun crews on to achieve faster and faster reloading times. He cursed them for being no better than a mob of snail-eating

Frenchmen, telling them that the Royal Navy prided itself on firing five shots to the Frenchmen's three, and that he was going to get them up to that standard if he had to kill half of them to do it. The experienced hands worked the guns bare-footed with a sweat rag around their foreheads.

For the Midshipmen, there were classes lasting an hour or two each day. Most attention was paid to navigation and seamanship, the lessons which were taught by the Master. We took daily sightings on the sun at noon with our sextants, worked out our position and kept our own logs which were inspected by the Captain once a week. We were instructed by the Boatswain or one of his mates in making knots, splices and lashings, or sent aloft to exercise in making or taking in sail, or instructed in heaving the lead. This meant heaving a weighted line ahead of the ship to discover the depth of water between us and the sea- bed. The Gunner put us through our paces with the cannon and carronades, explaining how the guns were rigged for running out, as well as the theory of naval gunnery. At other times the Marine sergeant showed us how to handle, load and fire the musket and the pistol, and one of the Petty Officers gave us cutlass drill.

I was attached to Mr Rawnsley, the Third Lieutenant,

for my watches. He was friendly, humorous and gave me encouragement. He set me the duties of heaving the log, by which our speed was measured. I was to mark the slate with the times and details of any change of course made, variations of wind direction, and make sure the next Officer of the Watch was called in good time. The log was a piece of wood with vanes that was kept stationary in the water, pulling out a light cord when it was dropped over the stern. The line was knotted at precise intervals so that within a timed period of, say, seven or fourteen seconds, the watchkeeping officer could count the number of knots passing through his fingers. If the number was five, the ship was travelling at five nautical miles per hour, or five "knots".

By the end of March, I was feeling fitter and healthier than at any time I can recall, whatever spare flesh I had having been turned into muscle by the constant exercise. The ship's mails arrived regularly, including several welcome letters from my family and a number of up-to-date news sheets.

"I say," said Octavius, glancing up from one of the latter, "d'you remember that General Bonaparte somehow managed to escape from Egypt to France last October?"

I nodded.

"Well," he continued, "he's been appointed the First Consul of France, it says here."

"Ruthless sort of character, ain't he?" commented Jem Ainsworth. "I wouldn't give much for the chances of the other Consuls, whoever they are."

"He won't be satisfied until he has made himself king," said Octavius sagely.

"Oh, I don't know about that," said Gerard. "The French have just chopped off the head of one king – what would they want with another?"

April – May, 1800

At the end of March we were told that the convoy we were to escort to the West Indies and North America had started to assemble. Early in April we joined it in the Solent. We formed part of the escort for some 40 merchant ships of different sizes, laden with tea, cloth, pottery, ironware and manufactured goods of every kind for sale in the Indies or the southern United States. Sailing singly would have been extremely dangerous for them, for they were easy prey for any prowling enemy warship or privateer. However, by sailing together it was possible for them to receive the protection of the Royal Navy.

While visiting the Liverpool waterfront with my father, it did strike me how round and tubby merchantmen were compared to a ship of war like the *Norseman*, but then they were built for a different purpose, namely to stuff as much paying cargo as possible into their holds. Although they were armed with a few popguns each, they were no match for a serious opponent. The escort consisted of ourselves, another frigate, the *Medusa*, somewhat larger than us and armed with 32 guns, and the smaller sloops *Crab* and *Otter*, of eighteen guns each. Captain Chant of the *Medusa*, being the senior officer, was in command overall. The two sloops, being small ships, did not carry sufficient rations and fresh water for the whole voyage and relied upon us to keep them supplied. Mr Occlestone, our Purser, was not pleased, for every inch of his stores was now filled with the additional supplies needed. He made representations to the Captain, saying that the fighting efficiency of the ship would be impaired if more had to be stored on deck. After discussions with Captain Chant it was agreed that some of the merchantmen must share the burden. Their Masters grumbled but had no option other than to agree.

We made but slow progress, for the pace of a convoy is that of the slowest ship. The merchant ships kept no sort of order together, especially at night, when they were fearful of collisions. Harry them as we might, they took no notice. At first, we took advantage of the north-easterly trade winds, which carried us south across the Bay of Biscay, down the coasts of Portugal and Spain, past the island of Madeira and the Canary Islands, where we paused within sight of land for the sloops to replenish their supplies. We then picked up a fine wind that pushed us steadily westwards across the Atlantic. The further south we went the warmer it became.

Boredom was our worst enemy. Recognizing this, one evening the Captain ordered Hands to Dance and Skylark, which meant that the entire ship's company was to entertain itself on deck, offering a prize of one guinea to the man judged by all to have performed the best Hornpipe. The performers folded their arms and danced only with their legs and feet in a bewildering series of steps as the fiddler played. The winner was chosen and accepted his prize to general applause. Other men sang songs or gave us tunes on the penny whistle, I got out my flute and Jem got out his violin. There was beginning to be a good feeling about the ship.

Two nights later we had a strange experience. The convoy was some distance ahead of us. Before he turned in, the Captain had decided to allow us plenty of sea room because of a heavy mist extending upwards to the topsail yards, the wind being barely sufficient to stir it, and so avoid the danger of a collision. The masthead lookout reported a ship about a quarter of a mile to starboard, where none should have been. I was sent aloft to confirm the report and, as the lookout had said, three masts could be seen protruding from the fog, moving very slowly northwards.

"What do you think?" asked Lieutenant Rawnsley when I returned to the deck. "Is he a merchantman or a man o' war?"

"I'm not sure, Sir. Only his topgallant masts are showing."

"Very well. You'd better wake the Captain."

I ran down to the Captain's cabin, knocked and went straight in. The cabin was lit by a single candle. It was clear that although Captain Montague had been sound asleep, he was fully awake and alert as soon as I had entered.

"Yes, Mr Grant – what is it?" he said.

"There's a strange sail to starboard, Sir," I replied. "She could be a man o' war, but we can't tell because of the mist."

"Very well, I'll come on deck," he said, reaching for his breeches. "Wake the other officers and tell them to send the hands to Quarters. Impress upon them I want no noise of any kind."

"Aye aye, Sir!"

When I returned to the Quarterdeck, Captain Montague was already there and had given the helmsman orders to steer towards the stranger. From all around came the patter of bare feet as the crew ran to their guns in the darkness.

"Mr Grant, go aloft and find out what our friend is up to, if you please," said the Captain.

I did as I was bidden and joined the lookout.

"He's turning away, Sir!" he said, pointing.

Sure enough, the gaps between the three distant masts were narrowing steadily until only the mizzen mast was visible, indicating that the other ship's stern was now towards us. Then, the stranger faded into the mist and vanished. I returned to the deck and informed the Captain, who made no comment. Slowly, we reached the point where he had last been seen, but we neither saw nor heard anything save five ghostly chimes of a distant watch bell. Fog plays strange tricks with sound, so while some said it came from dead ahead, others said that it was to port and others to starboard. We searched until dawn, when the fog bank rolled away to the north, taking its secret with it. All that could be seen were the distant masts of the convoy on the western horizon.

The Captain, who seemed to have been relishing the prospect of action and looked disappointed, told Mr Dacres to stand down from Quarters.

"Whoever it was evidently wished to remain anonymous," he remarked. "If we could see his topgallant masts, then obviously he could see ours, and he certainly sheered off the minute he saw us turning towards him. My guess is that he was a blockade runner – what's your opinion, Mr Dacres?"

"I think you're probably right, Sir," replied the First Lieutenant. "Our blockade of the French ports is so tight that almost nothing can get in or out. Still, there are always plenty willing to take the risk because if they do get through they can charge what they want for their cargoes."

"Yes, he could have been a French Indiaman," mused the Captain. "That would have given him the look of a frigate and he'd be well enough armed to give us a run for our money. Pity, really, as we could all have used the prize money. A cargo of tea, silks and spices would fetch a pretty penny."

Uncertain what the Captain meant, I asked Gerard to explain.

"Well, she might just have been a ship belonging to the French East India Company, making a run for home. If we had captured her, we would have been awarded prize money to the value of the ship and her cargo. The Captain's share would have been three eighths, the Lieutenants would have shared an eighth equally between them, and so on according to rank. The ordinary seamen and Marines would have shared one quarter, divided equally."

He paused for a moment, chuckling.

"That is why, when we go into action, you'll hear the seamen say they hope the enemy's fire will be divided in the same proportion as the prize money, that is, with the greater share going to the officers!"

Evidently the theory that the mysterious stranger had been a French Indiaman did not satisfy the crew. I heard mutterings among them that we'd just had a brush with the ghost of Captain Van der Decken and his ship the *Flying Dutchman*. According to legend, his ship was doomed to roam the seas for ever because of some pact or other he'd made with the Devil. No good would come of it, said some, and the Catholics among us crossed themselves.

On 3rd May the convoy divided, *Medusa* and *Otter* veering away to the north with most of the merchant ships, which were bound for the United States, where they would land one cargo and pick up another, leaving *Norseman* and *Crab* to look after the remaining eighteen. I had been so used to seeing them that I felt a sudden sense of loneliness as their topsails vanished beneath the horizon, the more so as the Captain had ordered even greater watchfulness from the lookouts as we were entering what he considered to be a danger zone in which the enemy could appear at any minute. I began to wonder whether our strange experience had been an ill omen after all, but kept these thoughts to myself as I did not wish to be thought a superstitious idiot by the others.

Nevertheless, it was soon after dawn two days later that the lookout reported three sail to the west. Shortly after, he shouted that they had altered course and were steering towards us. Captain Montague, suspecting that their intentions were hostile, promptly ordered Beat to Quarters. As I reached the Quarterdeck he was watching our Marine marksmen climbing towards the tops with their muskets slung around their backs. He turned to me and remarked that whilst he would undoubtedly require my services as messenger, I should not stand too close to him since he was a prime target, and such was the musket's lack of accuracy that any shot aimed at him would probably hit me! It would, therefore, be wise for me to keep moving when the battle commenced. I had never seen him as relaxed and agreeable – the prospect of action seemed to please him greatly.

The three approaching ships had now divided. Two of them – one about the size of one of our sloops (which the French call corvettes) and the other what seemed to be a topsail schooner – were heading straight for us, one on each bow, their clear intention being to make us divide our fire while they battered us from all directions. The third ship, also a corvette, was making directly for the convoy, clearly hoping to snap up prizes, but evidently hadn't spotted the *Crab*, lying behind and downwind of the lumbering merchantmen. There was now total silence aboard the *Norseman*. The guns had been loaded and run out, with their crews standing beside them. Most faces were turned towards the Quarterdeck, anticipating the next command, but a few of the more curious were peering through the ports at the oncoming enemy, above whose sterns I could see floating the red-white-and-blue flag of France. Most of our seamen had stripped off their shirts and tied sweatbands around their foreheads, as we were already beginning to feel the heat of the day. There was a sudden puff of smoke from the bow of the nearest corvette, a splash as the ball skidded off the water

100 yards short of us, then a ripping noise as it passed overhead, punching a hole through a sail.

"Eager for the fray, is he?" said Captain Montague dryly. "Well, I'll soon knock the damned enthusiasm out of him!"

I was suddenly afraid. My mouth was dry and tasted brassy. At home I had seen plenty of seamen with hooks instead of hands or peg legs to replace those lost in the service of their country, to say nothing of the blindness and terrible scars left by flying wood splinters. "The best cure for a headache is a cannon ball," the Gunner had once joked. "Trouble is, it takes your head with it!"

Despite the heat I felt an icy trickle run down my spine. At that moment I would rather have been anywhere else in the world. A voice inside me said that it was absurd to take part in the killing of Frenchmen I had never seen and who had done me no harm. Then it was sharply replaced by another that said these same Frenchmen were doing everything in their power to kill me, and I had better do something about it. I pulled myself together – I simply could not show myself to be afraid or let the ship down in any way. The Captain's voice broke in upon my thoughts...

"Mr Grant, kindly convey my compliments to Mr Dacres and tell him that he may reply with the bow chasers. I should be obliged if he would confine his fire to the enemy's hull."

Glad of something to do, I raced forward to the forecastle. As I did so, there was a crash overhead and a tangle of ropes and blocks dropped on to the netting. On my way back I looked up and saw one of the staysails was hanging loose. Suddenly, my fear was replaced by anger, for I had worked upon it myself and it had been a difficult job which would now have to be done again. When I reached the Quarterdeck the Captain was talking to the Master.

"I intend ignoring yon pipsqueak," he said, indicating the schooner. "He knows his thin timbers won't stand more than a shot of two from our carronades, so he'll stay as far as he can out of harm's way. As to our other friend, I'll meet him bow-to-bow. Of course he'll turn away with the wind behind, hoping to rake us through the bow with every gun in his broadside. We'll follow, depriving him of the chance, and then we'll be running parallel. After a couple of broadsides, we'll back topsails, cut across his stern and rake him, then finish the job by running close to his port side."

"Aye aye, Sir!" replied the Master and hurried away to warn the men at the braces. Our bow chasers were now banging away, their crews cheering as their shots sent splinters flying from the enemy's hull. We were now closing rapidly on the corvette. As predicted, she swung suddenly to port, her broadside guns firing in turn on the upward roll of the ship as they bore upon us, their balls tearing through our sails and rigging, where they caused considerable damage.

"Hard a'starboard!" ordered the Captain. *Norseman* began swinging on to a parallel course to the enemy, now only 50 yards distant. "Midships!"

"Fire as we bear, Sir?" shouted Lieutenant Emerson, commanding our port battery of guns. This meant that each gun would fire in turn as it bore on the target.

"No, fire together on my signal – I want to give that gentleman a lesson he will never forget!"

I felt something pluck at my coat tail. Musket balls from the marksmen in the enemy tops were cracking past. I remembered the advice I had been given and kept moving. I could see the French yelling and capering. Shouts of "*Vive la Republique!*" and "*A bas les Anglais!*" came across the water. Captain Montague was standing on a gun carriage, watching the enemy reload. As they were on the point of running out he shouted, "Now, Mr Emerson – fire!"

The port guns and carronades went off together in a mighty roar. Crashes and screams came from the French vessel, but the billowing smoke prevented us seeing the damage we had caused. Our own gunners were reloading like fiends. The second broadside was more ragged, but the result was the same. A few of the French guns replied and some of our men went down. For a moment their screams of agony made me freeze, then I somehow closed my mind to the sound.

"Bring her to, Mr Rowcroft! Quickly, now!" shouted the Captain. The topsail yards were heaved round to spill the wind from the sails, leaving them pressed against the masts and acting as a brake on our progress. As the ship lost way the enemy drew ahead. "Mr Grant, my compliments to Mr Rawnsley and tell him his guns are to fire as they bear. We are about to rake and when we have finished I do not wish to see a pane of glass left in the Frenchman's cabin windows."

I ran along the starboard battery shouting these instructions to Lieutenant Rawnsley. The gun crews grinned among themselves at the Captain's words.

"Braces, Mr Rowcroft! Hard a'port!" said the Captain, sharply.

"Come on, put your backs into it!" shouted the Master. "Heave her round, lads, that's the way!"

Creaking, the yards swung round and the topsails filled. As the ship gathered way again her head began to swing. Seeing his terrible danger, the Frenchman put his wheel to starboard but his rudder had barely started to act when, in rapid succession, our guns began firing through his stern. A raking such as this must be a fearful thing, for the balls travel the length of the ship, smashing everything in their path. Some of the carronade balls, fired on the downwards roll, must have torn holes clean through the corvette's bottom. The Captain returned us to a parallel course. At ten yards' range the port guns maintained a rapid fire to which the enemy made little reply. The corvette's mainmast tottered forward, dragging a tangle of rigging down with it. A minute or two later the tricolour flag was lowered.

The crew shouted their delight. "She's struck, boys! She's struck! Three cheers for the Captain!"

I joined in the cheering, but then the powder smoke drifted away on the wind, enabling us to see the terrible devastation we had wrought on our opponent. The schooner was already heading for the horizon but the sound of heavy gunfire from across the water indicated that the *Crab* was still heavily engaged with the second corvette. Lieutenant Dacres was therefore sent across to take possession of the surrendered vessel with a party of Marines and seamen while we steered towards the action. I steeled myself for the next round of the fight. Seeing our approach, however, the enemy broke away and followed the schooner. When we returned to our prize, which we saw was named *Sans Culotte*, she was low in the water with the sea already lapping the gun ports. The French crew and our own men were working frantically to extract the wounded from the smashed timbers and tangled rigging. Mr Dacres hailed that she was making water so fast that he doubted she would last another ten minutes. The remaining boats were sent over and everyone was taken off. Shortly after, the sea lapped over her bows and she went down, leaving all manner of flotsam to float to the surface.

I was standing beside the Captain when the only surviving French officer was brought aboard. He said that his name was Duroc and that he had been the *Sans Culotte*'s Second Lieutenant. He was of middling height, had a sallow complexion and one of his cheeks had been slashed open by a wood splinter. Speaking in excellent English, he told us that the enemy ships were based at Cayenne, a French colony on the coast of South America, and patrolled regularly in the hope of snapping up a British convoy, adding that we were small for a frigate and this had led his captain to underestimate our strength. Shrugging, he commented that such mistakes had to be paid for. He estimated that the *Sans Culotte* had sustained the loss of some twenty killed and perhaps twice that number wounded. I was sent to measure our own losses, which came to two killed and six wounded, two of them seriously. I was grateful that I had survived unharmed, but such elation as I felt at our victory vanished when I passed through the orlop, where I saw the terrible things that cannon shot can do to flesh and bone. The surgeon and his mates were hard at work upon British and French alike, sawing, stitching, probing and binding. Those for whom there was no hope were placed to one side and allowed to die quietly, while those with minor wounds were waiting their turn patiently. The screams of those upon the table I can never forget.

Returning to the Quarterdeck with my tally of dead and wounded, I found the Captain in conversation with Lieutenant Dacres. In his ironic way he commented that as the merchantmen for whom we had provided protection were doubtless grateful for our efforts, they should contribute a man apiece to make good our own losses and those of the *Crab*. Mr Dacres agreed, remarking that it would take the rest of the day to complete temporary repairs aloft, and that as the boats were already in the water he would instruct the officers to proceed immediately. This yielded a dozen seamen, both men and boys, after much grumbling from the ships' masters, who complained that they were already short-handed. Two of the French prisoners, natives of Cayenne, also volunteered. Our main topgallant mast was beyond repair, as were two of the yards. There were also sails to be patched and much rigging to be spliced or replaced.

We reached Barbados two days after the sinking of the *Sans Culotte*, and here responsibility for the merchant ships ended. As the facilities at Barbados were inadequate to enable us to complete repairs, we were directed to proceed to English Harbour in Antigua, where there was an excellent naval dockyard. On the way there we called at the island of Martinique, which had been captured from the French some time ago. Here, we were to refill our water casks, which had grown sour. The principal harbour of Martinique, as with of all these islands, was protected by magnificent fortifications. Any one of these would put our little fort at Liverpool to shame.

The Caribbean Sea is almost completely enclosed by land. At its eastern edge lie the Windward and Leeward Islands; to the north are the much larger islands of Cuba, Hispaniola, Puerto Rico and Jamaica; to the west and south are the coasts of Central and South America. The islands are beautiful, the climate hot yet cooled by sea breezes, and everywhere there are exotic fruits aplenty coupled with a pleasant smell of spices. Strange frigate birds circled our masts while we were close to land and pelicans eyed us curiously. I saw, too, shoals of flying fish and dolphins that played beneath the ship's bows as though they wanted to show us the way. When I looked down into the sea it was often so clear that I could see the sandy bottom, many fathoms below. Once, I watched an enormous turtle rise from the depths, poke his head out of the water to look at us, then, having decided that we were not very interesting after all, sink to the bottom again.

While ashore on ship's business in Antigua I met an officer of the 64th Regiment and remarked that the Garden of Eden cannot have been very different from the Caribbean. He laughed, saying I had yet to see a hurricane come roaring in from the Atlantic, turning buildings into matchwood and flattening plantations, to say nothing of the accompanying tidal waves that will carry a full-rigged ship up to a mile inland. And then, he added, there was always the presence of Yellow Jack, the dreaded Yellow Fever that cost his regiment the lives of 50 men a year.

We took it in turn to dine with the officers of the regiment in their mess on Shirley Heights. This was sited on a hilltop with a magnificent view over the harbour and caught whatever cooling breezes there were. It also had a pleasantly shaded verandah on which the mess's African servants served an excellent rum punch.

After completing our repairs we proceeded to Port Royal in Jamaica. It was every bit as much a Navy town as Portsmouth and was commanded by Rear Admiral Lord Hugh Seymour, who came aboard and dined with the officers. Captain Montague was less than pleased that we were under his command as one-third of his own share of any prize money earned goes to the Admiral as a matter of course. He commented that admirals could become very rich indeed without leaving their armchairs.

While most of the crew were replenishing our munitions I caught a man stealing from another's sea bag and was witness against him when he came before the Captain. He was a sly little fellow with sharp, darting eyes and was one of those we took off the merchantmen. He had no defence as I found the items in his possession. The Captain awarded him 50 lashes, at which the fellow foolishly argued that it was beyond his power to award more than 36. The Captain damned him for a sea-lawyer and told him the additional fourteen were for his impudence. The man howled throughout his punishment, which the crew believed to be well-deserved.

The news reaching Port Royal from Europe was that General Bonaparte had inflicted a crippling defeat on our Austrian allies at a place called Marengo in northern Italy. The general opinion seemed to be that as he had become virtually dictator of France we were likely to be hearing a lot more of him.

After four weeks at Port Royal we sailed for Hispaniola. Mr Rowcroft, the Master, was familiar with the island. He told me that it was divided into two parts. The larger, eastern portion was called Santo Domingo and was a Spanish possession in name only, while the smaller western part was known as Saint Domingue and belonged to France. When the French revolutionaries in Paris proclaimed Liberty, Equality and Brotherhood for all men, the slaves in Saint Domingue took it that these beliefs applied to them too, and rose against their masters, who had treated them with greater cruelty than anywhere else in the Caribbean. A many-sided civil war had followed, fought between the supporters of the French King and those who favoured the new Republic, and between slaves, whites and mulattos. It had spread across the frontier until a similar situation existed in Santo Domingo as well. British troops sent from Jamaica had prevented the anarchy spreading to our own possessions, but Yellow Jack had claimed the lives of so many that they had to be withdrawn. A former slave called Toussaint L'Ouverture, a man of intelligence, honour and ability, had now brought the situation under control and curbed the wilder elements of all parties. Nowadays, Mr Rowcroft said, there were few French or Spanish warships to be found in these parts, but enemy privateers, many of them little better than pirates, were present in some numbers, preying upon our merchantmen then concealing themselves among the many hiding places among the islands.

The privateers were elusive. We sighted several sail, but all seemed to recognize us for what we were and made off quickly. On 2nd September, however, we took one of them, a French ship named *Rivoli* of ten guns and 75 men. On rounding a point near the eastern end of Santo Domingo we found her alongside a prize she had just taken, the *Alan Adair* out of Bristol, laden with general cargo. The French, being too busy a'plundering, were in no position to defend themselves and surrendered at once. They refused to disclose their hideaway, but their commander, a M. Clausel, was unable to produce his Letters of Marque, which gave him and his men official status as combatants. When he discovered this, Captain Montague smiled coldly and promised to hang them one by one from the yardarm as pirates, at which they told us everything we wished to know. They told us that their lair was within a landlocked bay, the Bahia de San Cristobal, on the west coast of Puerto Rico. When they left it three days earlier, it contained two privateers, the French *Dangereuse* of eight guns and 60 men, and the Spanish *Conchita* of six guns and 40 men, plus two captured merchantmen they had brought in. All usually preyed upon British ships using the Mona Channel, between Puerto Rico and Santo Domingo. Not wishing to be burdened with prisoners, we kept only the officers and, having flung the small arms of the rest into the sea, set them ashore to take their chances on land.

The Captain decided upon a plan to raid the privateers' lair. At dawn in two days' time the *Rivoli*, flying French colours, would be seen leading her prize, the *Alan Adair*, into the bay. Both ships would have strong boarding parties from the *Norseman* concealed aboard them. The *Rivoli* would first come alongside the *Dangereuse* and board her with half the men aboard, then do likewise with one of the captured merchantmen, using the other half. Likewise, half of those aboard the *Alan Adair* would board the *Conchita* and half the second merchantman. Each of the four boarding parties would be divided into three groups – one to drive the enemy below and batten them down, one to cut the anchor cable and one to make sail. My task would be to lead the party making sail aboard the *Dangereuse*. Meanwhile, the *Norseman*, with only a skeleton crew left aboard, was to lie concealed in the lee of a wooded island a mile or two along the coast, but make sail for the bay's entrance at dawn, timing her arrival to cover the escape of the ships we intended to capture.

Some of the officers believed that the plan, while daring, was too ambitious and contained too many risks, pointing out that so few hands would be left aboard the *Norseman* that if anything went seriously wrong she would cease to be a fighting ship. The Captain thanked them for their thoughts but replied that, in his opinion, the element of surprise would be too great for the enemy to react quickly. In one way, I was pleased that, for the first time, I had been entrusted with a really important task. In another, I was only too conscious of the risks involved, especially clambering about the rigging of a strange vessel in semi-darkness.

Dusk on 3rd September found us anchored in the lee of the wooded island near the Bahia de San Cristobal. At midnight those of us who formed the boarding parties were transferred to the *Rivoli* and the *Alan Adair*. By dawn we were off the entrance to the harbour, the mouth of which is concealed by a jutting headland. We were flying the French flag and made every show of being pleased with ourselves at having taken a prize. A few men waved at us from the shore. Our Marines in their scarlet coats were concealed below. We quickly identified the *Dangereuse*, bumped alongside, and over we went on to her deck, led by Lieutenant Dacres.

It was ill luck that she was at that moment preparing for sea, for after they had recovered from their first surprise, the Frenchmen, who outnumbered us, came pouring out of their hatches. By then, some of my party were hauling up the jib at the bows while the rest of us scurried aloft to loose the foretopsail. As the anchor cable had already been cut with an axe, the vessel began to gather speed slowly. The deck below was crowded with fighting men, the clash of cutlasses and bang of firearms mingling with the screams of those who had received their death blow. The Marines were plying their bayonets and butts vigorously but the French were too many for us and we were being steadily forced back towards the bows.

I descended to the forecastle deck to find Armstrong, the brutal-looking seaman who had been flogged at the beginning of our voyage, thrust back against the rail by three Frenchmen. He was defending himself with difficulty against their cutlasses, and would surely have been killed had I not shot one of his assailants with my pistol and stabbed the second in the arm so hard with my dirk that he yelped and dropped his cutlass. Armstrong cut down the third quickly. I saw him look at me strangely, and then I was felled by a blow to the head from the butt of a French musket. For a few minutes I lay stunned, conscious only of the sounds of fighting and the feeling of being trampled underfoot. Then the deck gave a lurch, there was the sound of cheering and the fighting ceased.

When I came to, all four ships were heading for the harbour entrance, outside which lay *Norseman*, as the Captain had promised. It seems that *Rivoli*'s second boarding party had secured their merchantman without a struggle and, seeing our own difficulties, had brought her alongside and attacked the enemy from the rear. Some of the French dived overboard, others dashed below and the rest threw down their arms. The Spaniards aboard the *Conchita* had swum for the shore after putting up a brief fight, and the second merchantman had also been recovered without difficulty.

With prize crews now manning our various captures, we set sail for Port Royal, covered by the guns of the *Norseman*. The Captain gave the order to splice the mainbrace, which meant an extra issue of grog in recognition of the crew's efforts. The seamen were in understandably high spirits, talking of how they would spend their prize money. The mood in the Midshipmen's berth, however, was more restrained, for Jem Ainsworth had been shot dead almost as soon as he boarded the *Dangereuse*. Eight of the seamen and Marines had been killed, and twice as many wounded. Lieutenant Dacres received a painful gash from a boarding pike, which is a sort of spear, along his ribs, but it would heal. So would my head, which ached horribly. It had a huge egg-shaped bump upon it and was bandaged, having bled considerably. Pedro doubted if my shirt could be laundered, so stained was it. Privately, I was worried by the fact that I had killed a man, and had done so without a moment's hesitation.

"You didn't have much choice, did you?" said Gerard when I confided in him. "If you hadn't, then Armstrong would have been killed and you'd have had his death on your conscience, which would have been worse." I decided he was right and that I must learn to live with such things when a war is being fought.

On the morning of 10th September our little convoy, flying our own flags above those of the enemy, was cheered into Port Royal. The Admiral came aboard and made a rousing speech to the crew, as well he might since he would benefit handsomely from our efforts. The seamen auctioned the possessions of those who were killed, the modest proceeds being held in trust by the Captain for their families.

We returned to our cruising station off Santo Domingo, and week followed week without incident. But then came the horrifying discovery that we had Yellow Jack aboard. Lieutenant Seward and five of the hands were sent to the Naval Hospital at Port Royal when next we put in there for supplies. Although far fewer seamen seemed to die of the disease than soldiers, Captain Montague would not risk its spreading in the confined space of the ship. The older hands said that the hospital was simply a place in which to die, but the truth was that some men did recover, and once they had done so they did not get the disease again.

Christmas again found us at Port Royal. In the Midshipmen's berth we celebrated with freshly killed roast pork, shared with the Gunroom. Pedro made us a fine plum pudding, save that it contained no plums, although there was plenty of treacle in it and not a little rum. Afterwards, I felt badly out of sorts and decided to sling my hammock early.

On the day following Christmas I had awakened with a severe headache which spread to my limbs and back. Later, I began to shiver and sweat alternately and to vomit black bile. The surgeon said it was Yellow Jack. I was brought ashore to the hospital, but remember little of that time save disturbed dreams from which I awoke drenched in sweat and babbling. It was expected that I should die, so much so that the hospital staff went through my sea chest, which had come ashore with me, to find my parents' address so that they could be notified of my death. Luckily, they found a letter of introduction that Father had given me to a Jamaican merchant, Mr Jeremiah Morris, with whom he did much business. Duties had prevented me from calling upon Mr Morris, but as soon as he had been advised of the position he removed me from the hospital to his house on the hills outside Kingston. There, in a spacious airy bedroom in January 1801, I was nursed by Mrs Morris and her servants for many days. Dr Cairns, Mr Morris's family physician, said that if the hospital surgeon had been allowed to go on bleeding me for much longer I should certainly have died. Instead, he administered a mixture of local tree bark, wine and laudanum, giving instructions that I was to be kept as cool as possible. Finally, the fever broke, enabling me to drop into a long, untroubled sleep.

I was very weak and had lost much weight. My skin and the whites of my eyes had become a startling yellow, but I was told that they would assume their normal colour in time. Mr and Mrs Morris, who were about my parents' age and had lived in Jamaica for many years, showed me much kindness and said that I must not consider returning to duty until Dr Cairns declared me fit to do so. In the meantime I was introduced to the island's social life and taken about to parties and balls, feeling somewhat foolish as my uniform now hung upon me like a scarecrow, although I made a number of new friends. I discovered that not every African on the island was a slave. There were many freemen, as they were called, and such was the lack of hostility between the two races that it was possible to form the West India Regiment from them. The regiment was several battalions strong and its presence reduced the number of British troops required to serve in the islands. I encountered several of its members in Kingston and was able to observe that its uniform was much the same as that of our own infantry, although the soldiers wore soft shoes instead of boots. Having grown up barefoot, they were unable to march very easily in boots.

The London news sheets, which took weeks to reach us, contained good news. Russia, Sweden and Denmark, angered by our stopping their ships to search for contraband goods, had signed a pact called the Armed Neutrality of the North, designed to destroy our trade with the countries surrounding the Baltic. The effects would have been to break our blockade of France, deny the Royal Navy timber for masts and spars, and cut off vital supplies of grain. However, Admiral Nelson had broken this alliance by destroying the Danish fleet at Copenhagen on 2nd April. The action was so hard fought that at one stage Nelson's superior, Admiral Sir Hyde Parker, ordered him to withdraw. It is said that when Nelson's attention was drawn to this he raised his telescope to his blind eye, commenting that he really did not see the signal. He went on to win a tremendous victory. He seemed to have a sort of magic about him in the way he produced such astounding results and, once again, I found myself hoping that one day I should serve under him. I chuckled as I thought of Octavius and the wry manner in which he joked that because, like Nelson, he is of small stature and a clergyman's son, great things will be expected of him. Suddenly, I found myself wanting to be back aboard the *Norseman*.

Early in June, as soon as Dr Cairns declared I was fit enough, I reported for duty at Port Royal. The Admiral's staff would have assigned me to another ship, but at my request they agreed that I should return to the *Norseman*, which was daily expected to return from another cruise. A day later, I watched her come in, and although she was not the biggest or the smartest frigate in the world, she was my home and I thought she looked wonderful. I received a warm welcome aboard. Even the Captain shook my hand, which he had never done before, and while Lieutenant Dacres again looked with disapproval at my uniform, he simply laughed and said I should get some fat back on my bones. As Lieutenant Sewell did not survive the fever, the Captain had appointed Gerard Shipley Acting-Lieutenant, a temporary rank that did not apply outside the ship.

He, too, was pleased to see me, despite having acquired the air of reserve becoming of a lieutenant.

There were now just four of us left in the Midshipmen's berth. Keith Butler and Peter Dunn had long since given up treating Octavius as a figure of fun and, having been so long together, we had become used to each other's ways and got on well. While I was away, Octavius had taken to drawing cartoons of life aboard the *Norseman*. He was able to capture anyone's likeness in a few lines and the subjects were very funny. He told me that once, during Captain's Rounds of the ship, he had left one out. It showed a furious Lieutenant Dacres giving Keith a telling off. The Captain had handed it to Mr Dacres without comment, and Mr Dacres had sent Octavius to the masthead for the rest of that watch. This meant he had to cling to the top-most yard of the ship as she leaned and rolled with the sea. Mastheading was another form of punishment reserved for badly behaved Midshipmen – and a tough one if the weather was heavy. However, when Octavius returned to the deck, Mr Dacres simply warned him against making fun of senior officers, then purchased the cartoon for a guinea, saying that it would amuse his family. Our First Lieutenant, it seemed, was human after all.

On deck I came across Armstrong, the former convict, coiling down a rope with his huge hands. Straightening up, he towered over me, touching his forelock, which he did but rarely.

"Ah, Mr Grant, Sir, I'm glad to see you back," he said in his deep, powerful voice. "I just wanted to say I'm beholden to you for what you did during the fight aboard the *Dangereuse*."

"Why?" I asked. "It seemed to be the right thing to do at the time."

"Well, Sir, one way or another, the debt will be paid, for I'll not owe any man," he said. For a moment he looked thoughtful and then continued. "You see, Mr Grant, people are not always what they seem. Now you've always treated me fairly, so I'd be grateful if you could spare me a minute while I tell you about a friend of mine – just so that we can set the record straight, so to speak, Sir."

"Go on," I said, realizing that he wanted to tell me something about himself.

"Thank 'ee, Sir. Now when this friend of mine was aged ten, he was thrown out of the parish workhouse to fend for himself. He worked in fairs, where, as he grew older and his great strength became apparent, he learned the skill of bare-knuckle prize-fighting. It was something he was very good at and soon he was matched with the best in the country, earning large sums that he quickly spent. There were, however, always likely lads in the taverns who sought to make a name for themselves by provoking him, and in one such fight he had killed one of them. He had been tried for manslaughter but the judge, taking into account the fact that he had not struck the first blow, had offered him the choice of serving in the Royal Navy or going to prison. He was taken aboard a warship, but as he would acknowledge no man his master, he had tried to escape and been caught and punished. Yet, for all that, he's an honest man, Sir, and I'd like you to know that."

I understood that he was grateful to me, but I pointed out that in the Navy we each depend upon the other, so he did not owe me anything.

"Ah, now that's as maybe," he grunted, his battered face breaking into something resembling a grin. "Time will tell, Mr Grant, Sir, time will tell."

With that he knuckled his forehead again and walked away, leaving me with the impression that I had somehow acquired a personal bodyguard.

While I was ill the mail I received was usually out of date because it was addressed first to the ship, then re-directed to the hospital, who sent it on to the Morris's. However, at the end of July a letter from my father caught up with me and this contained more recent news.

My Dear James,
We are all giving thanks that you have recovered
from the Yellow Fever. Mr and Mrs Morris have kept
us informed of your progress and I have written
thanking them for all their kindness. I am told by the
town's leading medical men that having survived one
attack of this disease, it is unlikely that you will suffer
another, which is further cause for gladness.

All the family send you their love. Your mother
worries much about you although I tell her that we
should know soon enough if aught ill were to befall
you. Nevertheless, she hopes that now you are
recovered you will write as often as your duties

permit. Your brother Alexander now has a baby son whom he has called Mungo, after your grandfather. Your sister Ailsa's nuptials were a joyous occasion during which we danced away most of the night at the Assembly Rooms. She is now with child and is hopeful to be delivered of it at the year's end or thereabouts. Your sister Catriona continues to cause grief among her suitors. One of them, a pleasant young fellow whose father is a banker, went so far as to ask me for her hand in marriage. As he is suitable I said he is welcome to it, although he will have to persuade her on the subject and as yet she will give him no answer. However, she confides in her mother, who tells me that she simply wishes to keep the poor fellow dangling and will assent in the end.

Our business remains steady and would be good were it not for the war. Recently a cargo in which I had a share was lost when the ship was taken by a French privateer off the Carolinas. The insurance underwriters will, in their own good time, pay the cost price only, so we have to forego the profit we should have made, to say nothing of the loss of return on the capital involved, which we could well put to other uses while payment is awaited. I believe that the French and Spanish privateers are doing more damage to our trade than the combined navies of both nations.

I pray that you will be kept safe and hope that you will send us word of your doings when time permits. I remain, as always,

Your affectionate Father,
Hamish Grant

With the contents of Father's letter in mind, I was grateful for the chance to hit back when we were ordered to pay another visit to the Bahia de San Cristobal, as the privateers had again become active in the Mona Channel. When we arrived off the harbour entrance, we discovered that the Spaniards, enraged by the results of our last visit, had erected a fort on the headland, and that it contained a substantial number of heavy guns. For over an hour our guns were in continuous action against the fort, but as far as I could see we did it very little damage. Although we did not lose a man, the Spaniards' return fire cut up our sails and rigging so badly that we had to return to Port Royal for repairs.

Once these were complete, Lieutenant Holder of the Marines put forward a plan to destroy this nest of privateers. Captain Montague called all the officers to his cabin to discuss the details.

"During the bombardment I was observing the

fort's construction closely," said Holder. "In my opinion it is no different from any other coast defence battery. It has been built to withstand fire from warships, but not a determined attack from the landward side. In fact, I am sure that the landward defences will consist of nothing more than a ditch and a low wall containing a gate. We should experience no difficulty in scaling that wall during the hours of darkness."

"I agree with everything Mr Holder has said," commented the Captain. "His plan will require our being reinforced by the Marines from other ships presently in Port Royal, but I believe that the Admiral will agree to that. The essence of the plan is this. A strong landing party will be put ashore by night a mile or so up the coast from the entrance to the Bahia de San Cristobal. It will storm the fort from the landward side at dawn, then blow up the defences. Meanwhile, the landing party's boats will return to the ship to embark boarding parties, then row with muffled oars towards the harbour entrance. As the fort is being stormed the boarders will capture any vessels in the harbour. The boats will then pick up the landing party, and any prisoners taken at the fort, from the harbour entrance. Are there any questions, gentlemen?"

Everyone seemed to agree that the plan was a good one. On 7th August we were put ashore a mile from the San Cristobal headland two hours before dawn. The landing party's seamen were under the command of Lieutenant Rawnsley and I was to act as his second-in-command. We made our way quietly along the wooded slopes until we reached the edge of the trees, no more than 30 yards from the low wall of the fort. Rawnsley and Holder had agreed the form the attack would take. Using knotted ropes tied to grappling hooks, the seamen would scale the walls, silence the sentries and open the gates, through which the Marines would rush into the interior.

We could see two Spanish sentries patrolling the walls together, chattering noisily as they smoked their cigars, whiffs of which reached us whenever they passed nearby. At length, seeing them pause at the end of their beat, Lieutenant Rawnsley gave the signal for the seamen to advance. We made a silent rush forward, up went the grapnels to hook on to the wall's parapet, and then the seamen were swarming up the knotted ropes. The sentries, returning to investigate the noise, were felled immediately, although one managed to fire a shot that wounded a seaman.

My own task was to lead the group responsible for

opening the gates. We tore down the steps and into the archway. I was conscious that the guard room door had been flung open. Suddenly a voice shouted, "Mr Grant, Sir – look out!" I turned to see a Spanish soldier levelling his musket at me. Almost immediately, Armstrong knocked it upwards so that the shot passed over my head to thud into the gate. Then he picked up the man as though he were a doll and flung him bodily at the rest of the guard as they emerged from the door, felling them like so many skittles. As the seamen dealt with them I unbarred the gate and swung it open. The Marines charged into the courtyard to round up the rest of the confused garrison, who had emerged from the barrack block in their shirt-tails. Two Spanish officers, seeing that resistance was useless, surrendered their swords to Lieutenant Holder.

This time it was I who owed Armstrong my life. I shook his hand, commenting, "You're right – one good turn deserves another!"

He grinned, while from within his cavernous chest came a deep rumble that might have been a chuckle.

It was now light and the Marines had begun to drive spikes into the touch-holes of the enemy cannon, thereby preventing their being primed with powder and rendering them unusable. They also burned the wooden carriages of the guns for good measure. Sounds of fighting came from the harbour below, where we could see that the two enemy vessels within had already been captured and were moving slowly seawards while the boats pulled steadily for the tip of the headland, where they were to pick us up. Meanwhile, charges were being prepared to explode the fort's powder magazine. Backing away from its entrance across the courtyard, Mr Short laid a trail of gunpowder from a keg. "Get out of here, unless you want to stand your next watch with the Angel Gabriel!" he shouted, pulling a tinder box from his pocket. We needed no second urging. Seamen, Marines and prisoners alike raced down the track to the harbour mouth. As we were embarking in the boats there was a tremendous explosion, flinging chunks of masonry and timber bulks high into the air.

Once aboard *Norseman* it was possible to see that the fort had been reduced to a ruin. The smoke from the burning building remained visible for many miles out to sea. It has been a very satisfactory day with a modest butcher's bill – one man wounded at the fort, one man killed and five wounded during the cutting out.

This was to be the last action we fought for some time. During the autumn the first draft proposals for a peace treaty between the United Kingdom and the French and their Spanish allies were signed.

"I can't see Bonaparte wanting to keep the peace for long," commented Peter Dunn when the news was announced to the ship's company by the Captain.

"Why not? He's got what he wanted and become ruler of France – and he's got the Army behind him, which is what seems to count there," said Keith Butler.

"He's ambitious and not to be trusted," replied Octavius. "That's a dangerous combination. I think we'll find that France isn't big enough for him. He'll not be satisfied until he and his family rule most of Europe."

"Which, of course, means war again," added Peter. "He simply wants this peace as a breathing space to strengthen his hold on France itself."

I was inclined to agree with Octavius and Peter. After all, Bonaparte's record spoke for itself. It was not just that he had once served in the late King Louis' army then sided with the revolutionaries, for many decent men had done the same. Since then, though, he had shown no hesitation in abandoning his troops in Egypt so that he could return to France to seize the reins of power. Some of us also had doubts about the wisdom of some aspects of the peace treaty itself. For example, as far as the Caribbean was concerned, we were to return all the French and Spanish possessions we had taken, save for Trinidad, which made us feel that all our efforts had been for nothing.

Shortly before Christmas, Gerard Shipley finally passed the Examination for Lieutenant. He looked in to the Midshipmen's berth to say goodbye as he has been posted to another ship.

"Where are you bound?" I asked when we had congratulated him.

"I've been appointed Second Lieutenant on a sloop returning to England," he said with delight.

"That sounds good," I said.

"It is and it isn't," he replied. "When we get her home she will be scrapped and her crew paid off. After that I'll find myself ashore on half-pay, perhaps waiting for years for my next appointment, for as sure as eggs are eggs Their Lordships of the Admiralty will use the peace to reduce the size of the Navy and save money."

We wished him the best of luck. I was sorry to see him go, for he had been a good friend to me when I first came aboard. I imagined that one day, when I had passed the Examination for Lieutenant, I too might have to say goodbye to old friends and find myself looking for another ship.

Early in the year Lieutenant Dacres left us to take command of a brig, which is a small, fast, two-masted ship armed with sixteen guns, very useful for hunting down the faster privateers or carrying despatches. Lieutenant Emerson took over as our First Lieutenant. A new arrival, Lieutenant Thomas Allan, became Fourth Lieutenant. The Midshipmen's berth also received a new member, Adam Ward, who was sent to us to complete his six years' sea time as his own ship was returning to England. We found that he had not been trained as thoroughly as the rest of us and had much catching up to do. The Captain and Lieutenant Dacres had been hard taskmasters, but we had certainly learned our business.

Early in February we were cruising off Saint Domingue when a large French convoy came into sight. It seemed a little strange that, for the moment, the French were no longer our enemies. For a while we ran parallel with one of the escorting frigates, with whom we exchanged courtesies. Her captain told

Captain Montague that Bonaparte was not prepared to tolerate Saint Domingue being governed by former slaves and had sent his brother-in-law, General Victor Leclerc, with 25,000 men to re-establish French authority on the island. We were all doubtful whether this could be achieved, for Toussaint L'Ouverture, who had emerged as leader of the former colony's new government, was known to be a very capable general who had the support of the people.

The following month, as we were at peace and there were no privateers to chase, we were sent down once more to the English Harbour in Antigua for a refit. There we lived ashore while *Norseman* was hauled first on to one side and then the other so she could be careened. This meant scraping all the accumulated weeds and barnacles off her bottom as these reduced our speed by several knots.

With the Captain's permission, Peter Dunn set about organizing a cricket tournament between the various departments of the ship. This was great fun and thoroughly enjoyed by the crew. By picking the best players from each team, we eventually formed a ship's team, irrespective of rank, for which I was glad to be chosen, as I am a reasonable spin bowler. We challenged the 64th Regiment to a series of games, but as they are able to play all the year round they beat us easily at first. However, we practised hard and were able to beat them in the last game. The slaves loved cricket, which they played with gusto among themselves when they were not working. Crowds of them from the nearest plantations came to see our games after they had been to church on Sunday afternoons. Unlike English spectators, who respond to a good stroke or a good ball by clapping politely, they shouted and cheered and jumped up and down. They particularly liked Armstrong, our team's fast bowler, who could send down a ball so fast it was hardly visible, sending the stumps flying in all directions.

Having completed our refit, we returned to Port Royal at the beginning of August. After that we undertook a series of cruises around the Caribbean, either showing the flag by visiting our own islands or paying courtesy visits to those of our late enemies. The crew spent much time scrubbing the deck until it was white and polishing our already-gleaming brasswork so that we should give the best possible impression of our efficiency.

After all that had gone before, life was rather dull. My principal concern at this time was the amount I was having to spend on new uniforms at the Port Royal tailors, for I was growing so rapidly that a uniform ceased to fit me after only eight months.

By October, it was clear that matters were going very badly for the French on Saint Domingue. When they repossessed the islands of Martinique and Guadaloupe, they promptly restored slavery. This so alarmed the former slaves on Saint Domingue that they again took up arms, vowing to end for ever their connection with France. By falsely offering an amnesty, General Leclerc captured Toussaint L'Ouverture and shipped him off to France as a prisoner. But Leclerc himself was said to be suffering from Yellow Jack, while his troops, who were dropping in scores from the disease, were losing ground steadily to Toussaint L'Ouverture's successor, Jean Dessalines, a man noted for his ruthlessness.

❀ ❁ ❀

On 10th May 1803 we paid a courtesy visit to Santiago de Cuba, a fine deep harbour protected by excellent fortifications. We fired a salute and dipped our ensign as we entered, while the fortress guns banged away in return. The Captain and Lieutenant Emerson were received with much ceremony ashore and conducted to the Governor. That evening I was among those invited to dine aboard a Spanish ship of the line, the *Reconquista*, of 64 guns. The Spanish officers told us that they much regret the strong influence of France in the affairs of their country, which can do nothing but harm.

I was chuckling over a letter from Father telling me that Catriona has finally accepted her principal suitor's proposal when Keith entered our berth waving a recently arrived London news sheet.

"I say," he announced, "that fellow Bonaparte has had himself elected First Consul of France – for life, if you please!"

"That means he's just one short step from the throne," said Octavius. "We'll be in for trouble soon – it's only a matter of time."

Sure enough, on 15th June a fast frigate reached Port Royal from England. The despatches she brought informed us that, once again, we were at war with France. As we had predicted, Bonaparte had indeed used the recent peace as a means of strengthening his hold on power among his own people and now seemed set to resume his career of conquest. We were warned that, such was his influence over the Spanish court, Spain was likely to be hostile to us and would probably declare war on us again quite shortly. The news was received badly by those seamen who had been pressed into the service, for there had been talk that *Norseman* would be returning to England soon, and they had hoped to be paid off and receive their discharge. On the other hand, I was certain that the Admiralty would be forced to expand the Navy once more, and that meant that officers like Gerard and Lieutenant Dacres would not have had to spend too much time on half pay.

In July, Admiral Duckworth, now commanding the Jamaica station, ordered us to patrol the Windward Passage, across which the French troops were fleeing from Saint Domingue to Cuba. As we suspected they might, the Spanish authorities in Cuba had begun allowing French privateers free use of their harbours. The news from home, both in despatches and the London news sheets, was very serious, for Bonaparte had established a huge camp at Boulogne for what he called his Grand Army. Its purpose could only be an invasion of England. The seamen were unsettled by the news, saying that we should be sent home to assist in the defence of our country, but were reassured when the Captain told them that the Channel Fleet was quite capable of dealing with the threat.

The next five months were among the busiest of my entire time aboard *Norseman*. We captured, sank or drove aground no less than five French privateers in this period, the smallest had two guns, the largest twelve. We also intercepted a number of transport ships evacuating French troops from Saint Domingue to Cuba. The troops themselves, in their ragged, dirty uniforms, were a sorry sight. There was no fight left in them, but if we allowed them to reach safety they would soon recover and become our enemies once more, for Spain had once again allied herself with France and declared war on us. I was much away in the boats, taking possession of our prizes. Finding prize crews to take the captured vessels into Port Royal left us so short-handed that we retained a small schooner, the *Jeanne-Marie*, as a tender, giving command of her to Lieutenant Allan. The tender collected our prize crews from Port Royal and brought out supplies that enabled us to remain at sea for longer.

On one occasion we came up alongside a brig flying the red-and-green flag of Portugal. As two of the Lieutenants and the rest of the Midshipmen were absent aboard prizes, Captain Montague said that Octavius and I should lead the boarding party. It was rare to find a Portuguese ship in these waters and when I examined her carefully through my telescope I spotted something unusual.

"She's not what she seems, Sir," I said. "She's fitted with gunports, but they've been painted over recently to give the impression she's harmless. I'd like to take Pedro, the Steward, over with us. He's from Gibraltar and speaks fluent Spanish – the language is similar to Portuguese, so he should be able to make himself understood."

"We might make a Lieutenant of you yet, Mr Grant," said the Captain with a nod of approval.

We took a dozen burly, well-armed seamen with us, including Armstrong, who seemed to have appointed himself my bodyguard, and Richard Corbett, who had first shown me my way round the rigging when I joined the ship and had recently been promoted to Petty Officer.

We clambered aboard the brig to be met by a swarthy man who said he was her skipper and could speak a little English. His crew stared at us indifferently.

"You're a long way from Portuguese waters, Captain," I said. "What brings you here?"

He spread his hands, indicating the untidy piles of fishing nets, boxes and bales that cluttered the deck.

"We are poor men – we must earn our living where we can," he replied. "Sometimes we do a little fishing, sometimes we carry cargo between the islands.

"Let's see what's under all that clutter, shall we?" I said to Corbett, pointing to the nets and boxes. He and his men quickly uncovered six 18-pounder guns.

"You're heavily armed for poor fishermen, aren't you?" I commented, at which the skipper shrugged.

"There are many bad men in these times. We must defend our ship – she is all we have."

"There's a 9-pounder bow chaser up here, Sir!" shouted Corbett from the forecastle.

"Well now," I said, "bow chasers are for chasing other people's ships and knocking holes in them, aren't they? What do you say to that, Captain?"

"No understand," was all the reply I got. From the corner of my eye I saw Octavius whispering in Pedro's ear. Pedro suddenly addressed the brig's captain in Spanish. The man looked puzzled, then nodded.

"*Si*," he said.

"I asked him if his mother still steals clothes from

112

washing-lines," said Pedro, smiling with satisfaction. "He didn't understand and said yes. He is not Spanish or Portuguese, Sir."

Without warning, Octavius jabbed his dirk into the man's bottom.

"*Nomme d'un chien!*" bellowed his enraged victim.

"Here's a nice old Portuguese saying for you," remarked Octavius dryly. "Every dog barks in his own language! You're French, and you're either a pirate or a privateer. Doesn't matter much either way, because now you're a prisoner, old chap."

"There's a lot of shuffling going on between decks, Sir," called Armstrong. "Shall I have this hatch cover off?"

I told the rest of our boarding party to gather round the hatch with their muskets and pistols while the cover was removed. Below, blinking in the sudden sunlight, were 75 ragged soldiers, whom their officer said were anxious to escape from Saint Domingue to Cuba. While Armstrong and the rest were busy flinging the Frenchmen's muskets and other weapons overboard, I hailed Captain Montague and told him what had taken place.

"Very well, Mr Grant," he replied. "Take her in to Port Royal, will you? You seem to have earned your pay today."

This was high praise indeed, although I was alarmed by the sudden responsibility. The prisoners were battened down below deck with a warning of what would happen to them if they caused trouble. We had not far to go to reach Port Royal, and my navigation was now passable. Octavius stood watch with me. Although I half-expected the seamen to be concerned by having their lives placed in the hands of a couple of young Midshipmen, they seemed to trust us. Relieved as we were to deliver our charge when we reached harbour, Octavius and I felt well-pleased with our achievements, and just a little proud of ourselves.

After that, activity in the Windward Passage steadily decreased. This suggested that those French troops trying to leave Saint Domingue had already done so, or were holed up in the few well-fortified ports they still possessed. On 1st February 1804 we intercepted a small schooner crowded with French civilians, their wives and children. They said that Dessalines had ordered a massacre of all the remaining whites in Saint Domingue and were hoping that from Cuba they would be able to reach New Orleans which, though now an American city, contained a large French population. Having nothing but the clothes in which they stood and the few possessions they could carry, they posed no threat. Captain Montague therefore let them continue on their way. Despite their loss of a little prize money, our men approved, for Jolly Jack Tar has a soft heart and he hates to see children cry.

During the second week of March we were forced into the shelter of a bay by the worst tropical storm imaginable. The wind reached speeds I had never believed possible, whipping the tops off the waves so that we were almost blinded by spray. Normal speech was impossible, for words were simply blown away into the howling semi-darkness. Only by shouting directly into someone's ear could one make oneself understood. After several sails had been blown to tatters we were forced to run under bare poles, that is, without a stitch of canvas set.

Even in the bay our troubles did not end. The anchor refused to take hold and simply dragged its way across the bottom. At that moment we were being driven towards a rocky headland up which the surf was bursting well above masthead height. Had we gone aground at that spot, the ship would soon have been battered to pieces very quickly. Very few of us would have survived, for even those who managed to reach the shore would have been smashed to pulp against the rocks by those terrible breakers. Some of the men began to pray openly.

Finally, when we were just 50 yards from disaster, the anchor bit into a firmer piece of seabed. The ship jerked suddenly as the cable tightened, then her bows came round into the wind, steadying her. I ran forward, wondering whether the cable would take the tremendous strain placed upon it. Every fibre of the thick rope was groaning in protest, but it was holding and I gave thanks for the skill of the men who had made it. Nevertheless, I was pleased when the Captain gave the order for a second anchor to be dropped as a precaution.

To my amazement, within 24 hours, all trace of the storm had vanished. Once again, the Caribbean had become its calm, smiling self, with no hint of the terrifying forces that Nature had unleashed against us. We had sustained such serious damage to our sails and rigging that we had to proceed immediately to Port Royal and refit yet again. There we discovered that the storm had also sprung our mainmast so that it no longer stood at the correct angle. Our repairs therefore took a lot longer to complete than we had expected.

The mails from home provided a startling piece of news. Bonaparte had sat himself upon the throne of France and now called himself His Imperial Majesty Napoleon, Emperor of the French. The crew, who called him Boney, had become resigned to the prospect of a long war. I was particularly sorry for the married men with families. They had already been away from home for several years and from the conversations I heard they were greatly saddened by the fact that the children they left behind would be strangers to them when they did return.

We were back at sea at the end of August. On 22nd September, while on a northerly course off Guadaloupe, we were overhauled by a ship flying American colours. She was well armed and had an advantage over us of three or four knots. She deliberately passed close and up-wind of us, so that we were subjected to the most horrible stench of accumulated human waste and Heaven knows what else. Her crew, as nasty a crowd of gallows-bait as one could imagine, leered at us and shouted insulting remarks. In answer to being hailed, her master identified her as the *Good Fortune*, bound for the Carolinas with a cargo of African goods. He added insolently that it was about time we defeated the French once and for all so that honest seamen could earn a decent living again. Mr Short, puce with rage, told me that she was a Blackbirder, that is, a slave ship, and nothing would give him greater pleasure than putting a full broadside into her, save that it would be the poor wretches chained down aboard who would suffer most. We had, however, no authority to stop her and in any event she was capable of outrunning us with ease.

By Christmas 1804, I suddenly realized that five years had passed since I joined the Navy. During that time I had grown up a lot and learned much about people. I had learned that everyone is different and to make allowances for the fact. I had learned, too, that the seamen would work harder for you if they knew you were going to treat them fairly and keep them out of trouble, even if this sometimes meant turning a blind eye to their minor misdeeds, and also when to praise and when to reprimand. I had shed some illusions, too. On the deck of the *Dangereuse* at San Cristobal I had learned that there is nothing glamorous about hand-to-hand fighting, which is primitive, brutal and savage, although I also accepted that at times it could not be avoided.

Pardoe, the Gunner's Mate, had taken a tumble down a hatch during our last cruise, breaking an arm and a leg. He always had a smell of rum about him and was reputed to have his own supply, so it is possible that he was to blame for his own misfortune. We sent him ashore to the hospital in Port Royal. As Armstrong seemed to have settled down and was well regarded by the crew, I suggested to Mr Short that he should be up-rated. The Gunner agreed and Armstrong's promotion to Gunner's Mate was confirmed by the Captain.

Our cruises continued without incident until the morning of 20th May, when sail after sail broke the eastern horizon. A large number of ships was evidently making for the port of Santo Domingo, off which we were lying. As no movements of our own fleet were expected, we treated the new arrivals with great suspicion and alarm. Captain Montague took the precaution of taking us further out to sea, sending me to the masthead to observe. There was a stunned silence below as I reported that the newcomers were either flying the French tricolour or the scarlet-and-gold of Spain, counting them as they came up to drop anchor. At length my tally was complete. Within sight was an enemy fleet numbering eighteen ships of the line, seven frigates, four corvettes and numerous transport vessels.

When I returned to the deck the faces of the officers were grim. None could remember so great a concentration of enemy naval strength in the Caribbean and we wondered whether some disaster had taken place at home that permitted this. At length, Captain Montague decided that the enemy's intention might be to invade Jamaica and our first priority must, therefore, be to provide warning so that the island's defences could be put in order. We therefore put about and ran under all sail for Port Royal, where we arrived on the 25th.

The latest mails confirmed that no disaster had befallen the Channel Fleet, although our own news was received with the greatest alarm. We were ordered, with all speed, to convey despatches from the Governor to England requesting reinforcements, and also as much cash and bullion that the Jamaica merchants required transporting to safe keeping. To my mind, it seemed impossible that reinforcements could reach Jamaica before the French attacked, for even if sufficient troops could be mustered the passage of the Atlantic from England took weeks.

The Westerlies, which are winds that one can usually rely upon to provide a swift passage to England, were very weak. We had every sail set, but the delay tried the Captain's temper and we all suffered for it. No sooner had we dropped anchor in Portsmouth harbour on 28th June than he was off ashore in his gig. Shortly after, the shutters of the telegraph signal station on

Portsdown Hill began winking as fast as they could go. It seemed incredible that the news we brought would reach the Admiralty in less than an hour. It was good to see our green and pleasant land again after so long, though even in midsummer I felt it distinctly cool. In contrast to our own faces, tanned by sun and wind to the colour of mahogany, those of the local people seemed pale.

After taking on fresh supplies we were sent across the Channel to keep watch on the French naval base of Brest. It was possible to observe that the French squadron there was ready for sea, but it showed no sign of wishing to come out. We received news that the Franco-Spanish Combined Fleet we had encountered, returning across the Atlantic from the Caribbean, had been intercepted off Cape Finisterre by a British squadron. Two of the enemy ships were captured and the rest sought refuge in the port of Ferrol, on the north-eastern coast of Spain. Neither Octavius nor I could understand what the enemy's foray was intended to accomplish, for Jamaica was not attacked after all.

On our return to Portsmouth in September, we were told that the enemy's Combined Fleet had left Ferrol and moved south to Cadiz, on the southern Atlantic coast of Spain, near the Straits of Gibraltar.

Lord Nelson, who was commanding our blockading fleet there, had requested more frigates, and we were sent to join him. Day after day we observed Cadiz harbour, relaying signals through each other to the fleet, which lay just beyond the sight of land. Ward, the Midshipman who joined us in the Indies, had become an expert at sending and interpreting flag signals, whereas, unless I proceeded slowly, they sometimes meant as little to me as a line of washing.

On the evening of 19th October the enemy were perceived to be coming out of Cadiz. The wind was light and their progress was so slow that it took most of the following day for them to clear the harbour. Shortly after dawn on 21st October we were lying off Cape Trafalgar. The frigate captains were summoned aboard Lord Nelson's flagship, the *Victory*. We hove to within hailing distance of her and Captain Montague was rowed across. Having told the captains what was required of them, Lord Nelson saw them off at the gangway. I had been keeping my telescope trained on the flagship in the hope that at last I might catch a glimpse of him, but did not know he had appeared until the waiting boats' crews set up a shout:

"Hurrah for Lord Nelson, boys! Three cheers for the Admiral!"

Through the lens of my telescope I saw a slight man with longish grey hair, the empty right sleeve and the decorations pinned to his coat confirming that he was indeed Lord Nelson. I shall never forget the faces of the men in the boats as they looked up at him. He was their hero, they believed he would lead them to a great victory and they would do everything in their power to help him bring it about. He smiled at them, raising his left hand, turned and was gone. That was the first and only time I saw him.

Returning aboard, Captain Montague called the officers and warrant officers to his cabin. There he explained to us that Lord Nelson's plan was to break through the enemy line in two columns, one headed by himself in the *Victory* and the other by Vice-Admiral Collingwood in the *Royal Sovereign*.

"But surely, Sir, that means that for a while those ships alone will be exposed to the fire of the entire enemy fleet," Lieutenant Emerson interjected. "It will be murder aboard them!"

"The Admiral says it must be borne," replied Montague. "The first consideration is that as the rest of our ships arrive a general ship-to-ship engagement with the enemy will ensue, and in that our superior gunnery will prove decisive. The second is that by breaking the enemy's line in the centre, we deprive him of the advantage of superior numbers. For those ships at the front of the Franco-Spanish fleet can play no part in the fighting unless they reverse course towards the battle. This will be a very slow business for them as they will have to turn into the wind, which is presently too light to be of much use to them. Therefore, by the time they have come about, it will be too late for them to do any good. Hopefully, they will recognize this for themselves and head for safety before they too are overwhelmed."

The brilliance of the plan suddenly became clear and appreciative murmurs passed around the cabin.

"Our own role at this stage is simply to relay the signals of the frigate *Tenacious*, which is following the movements of the enemy fleet from closer inshore," commented the Captain in conclusion. "As those of you who have been present at a fleet action will already know, we shall not be closely involved in the fighting. A frigate has no place in a contest between line-of-battle ships – she cannot withstand the tremendous weight of fire they throw, nor can she do their stout hulls much damage. Nevertheless, we must be prepared for the unexpected and shall go to Quarters when the moment comes. When the battle is over we shall render assistance wherever it is needed."

After we had been sent to breakfast many of the crew went forward or aloft to catch their first glimpse of the enemy. I was nervous, as I always was before an action starts, but excited too, because at last we had a chance to deal a mortal blow to the French and Spanish Navies.

"Signal from *Tenacious*, Sir!" said Ward suddenly, his telescope to his eye. "Enemy has reversed course. New heading due north."

"Repeat!" snapped Montague, curtly. A line of flags was bent on to the hoist and soared aloft, relaying the news to our line-of-battle ships, now deployed in two columns heading east, with the *Victory* leading the port column. A shorter line of flags rose up the *Victory*'s halyards.

"Flagship acknowledges, Sir," said Ward. The Captain turned to me.

"Mr Grant, you'd oblige me by going aloft. Tell me when the enemy are within sight."

I pocketed my telescope and climbed to the masthead. The ship had a slow, ugly, corkscrew motion induced by an oily swell rolling in from the west. During my early days at sea such a movement would soon have made me violently sick, but now it was merely an inconvenience. The wind was light, so that to starboard the columns of our battle fleet were slopping along at no more than two or three knots. I settled myself and began scanning the eastern horizon. Already it was broken by the long line of the enemy's topsails, stretching from north to south, moving very slowly in the light wind.

"Well, Mr Grant?" shouted Montague. "We are all awaiting your observations with interest!"

"Enemy in sight, Sir! Twenty-eight – thirty – thirty-three sail, heading north!"

"Very well. Stay where you are for the time being and report any change. Beat to Quarters!"

Long practised as we were, the hustle and bustle of clearing ship and running out the guns was over very quickly. The *Victory* was informed of my estimate, which was confirmed by *Tenacious*. Now all we could do was wait as the distance between the two fleets slowly narrowed. Each minute dragged slowly past as anticipation took hold. Suddenly lines of signal flags began to rise on *Victory*'s hoists.

"General signal from flagship, Sir!" shouted Ward. "'ENGLAND EXPECTS THAT EVERY MAN WILL DO HIS DUTY.' Message ends, Sir."

Our men began to cheer, and from across the water came more and more cheering as the message was passed from ship to ship. As noon approached we were about 1,000 yards short of the wall of ships that formed the enemy fleet, with Collingwood's column some distance ahead of Lord Nelson's. Flame and smoke suddenly belched from the sides of the nearest French and Spanish ships as they opened fire, and to this *Victory* and *Royal Sovereign* could only reply with their bow guns. Another string of signal flags appeared in the *Victory*'s rigging.

"ENGAGE THE ENEMY MORE CLOSELY," read Ward. The Captain made no response. Distance prevented me from seeing the details but ten minutes later *Royal Sovereign* passed between two of the enemy ships, letting fly with a thunderous double-shotted broadside as she did so.

"Admiral Collingwood has broken the enemy line, Sir!" I reported. *Victory* was making much slower progress, although she had every sail set. I could see that she was taking a fearful hammering as, every minute, scores of French and Spanish guns blazed away at her. Her mizzen topmast toppled, bringing down miles of rigging with it, her foremast studding-sail booms were shot away and holes had appeared in all her sails. Yet, slowly and steadfastly, she continued to approach the hostile line, making what reply she could with her bow guns. It was not until one o'clock that she literally smashed her way between two of the enemy ships, into which she fired two tremendous broadsides. I could almost sense the relief aboard her as, at last, she was able to hit back and, to judge from the terrific rate of fire she was maintaining, she was hitting back very hard indeed. Almost at once she was surrounded by more of the enemy and I lost clear sight of her. I wondered how she could possibly survive, but then the next ships in Lord Nelson's column, *Temeraire*, *Neptune*, *Leviathan* and others, smashed their way in turn through the enemy and the action became general. The continuous thunder of gunfire rose to a crescendo. Then the scene was obscured by clouds of drifting powder smoke.

"Lord Nelson has broken through, Sir!" I shouted.

"Very well, Mr Grant," answered the Captain. "Keep the front and rear of the enemy line under observation and report developments."

I heard him give the order to heave to. The yards came round, spilling the wind from the sails, and *Norseman* slowed to a standstill just out of range of the enemy's guns, wallowing a little in the swell. More and more of the ships in Lord Nelson's column, *Conqueror*, *Britannia*, *Ajax* and *Agamemnon*, followed by *Orion*, *Minotaur* and *Spartiate*, were coming up in turn to add the weight of their gunfire to the fray. Beyond, I could see the ships of Admiral Collingwood's column similarly engaged. It was a tremendous spectacle that almost made me forget the task I had been given. I looked towards the front of the enemy line and, sure enough, five of their ships were turning slowly and heading back towards the fighting.

"Five enemy ships closing in from the north, Sir!" I reported.

The Captain gave the appropriate order to Ward and a string of signal flags soared up the hoists. Little could be discerned in the smoke save gun flashes and falling masts and, later, the dull glow of a ship ablaze. The thunder of guns was continuous. Evidently the five enemy ships to the north were having second thoughts about joining in the battle, for they unexpectedly altered course to the south-west. I reported this and we hoisted another signal. At about half past three I noticed that several ships from the centre and rear of the enemy line had broken away from the fighting and were heading north-east.

"Eleven of the enemy have broken off the action,

Sir!" I shouted. "They seem to be heading towards Cadiz!"

"Ha! They never could stand a close-quarter pounding match for long!" exclaimed the Captain, slapping his thigh with delight.

Ward signalled the news, but our message went unanswered by the *Victory*, as had the previous two. This did not necessarily mean that the flagship had not seen them, although they must have been difficult to read through the clouds of drifting powder smoke. The more probable explanation was the flagship's signal halliards had been shot away, so that she could make no response. At about four o'clock the firing died away and the smoke cleared to reveal a drifting panorama of shattered ships. Many of our own were dismasted or severely damaged aloft, but the French and Spanish were in a far worse state. As far as possible I counted how many of them had hauled down their flags in surrender.

"Seventeen of the enemy have struck their colours and one is burning to the waterline!" I called to those below, who sent up a tremendous cheer.

"A splendid day's work!" said Captain Montague, who was evidently in the best of humours. "Mr Grant, pray come down and join us!"

When I reached the deck he was giving orders for

the ship to get under way. We nosed in among the shattered ships and heaved to again. Octavius and I were ordered to take, respectively, the launch and the longboat and pick up survivors. As usual, Armstrong accompanied me. All round us, ships whose boats had survived the gunfire were doing likewise. I found myself close to the *Bucentaure*, the enemy's flagship, which had been reduced to a shattered hulk. Escorted by a British Marine captain, a French admiral was boarding another boat lying alongside.

"Who have you got there?" I called to a Midshipman in the other boat.

"Admiral Pierre Villeneuve, Commander-in-Chief of the Franco-Spanish Combined Fleet, no less," he replied, grinning. "His own boats have been smashed to matchwood, so when he surrendered we had to come and get him!"

As the Admiral settled himself in the boat's stern he glanced in my direction. The expression on his face was a mixture of despair and resignation. I felt sorry for him and raised my hat, as one does to any senior officer. He returned the compliment and then his boat pulled away.

"I wouldn't be in his shoes for all the tea in China," commented Armstrong, reading my thoughts. "There goes a man who'll have a deal of explaining to do when he gets home."

We picked our way through floating wreckage of every kind to rescue men clinging to it. Most were Frenchmen or Spaniards, but there were some of our own people as well. The rescue work continued until after dusk. It had become very dangerous, for the swell was rising and the wind was getting stronger by the minute. There was a very real chance that the boat would be holed by a spar or some other piece of wreckage floating just below the surface. We came across three Frenchmen hanging on to part of a mast sticking up out of the water at an angle. After they had been helped aboard, the mast, relieved of their weight, was lifted by a sudden swell and fell across our bows, forcing them under the surface. We were already overloaded and water poured into the boat.

"Bale!" I shouted as two men struggled vainly to lift the wreckage clear.

"Stand aside, mates!" said Armstrong, making his way forward through the packed boat. "Let the dog see the rabbit!"

Pushing the two men aside, he began to exert his mighty strength. Sweat broke out on his forehead and the muscles of his arms bulged. Slowly the mast began to rise.

"Next time the swell drops, go astern if you please, Sir!" he called, panting.

"Give way!" I shouted as we slid sluggishly into a trough between the waves. The oarsmen had already backed their oars. Slowly the boat began to move backwards. With a final heave Armstrong lifted the spar over the bows.

"Well done!" I said as he returned to his seat. "If it hadn't been for you we'd all have been swimming now!"

"Ah, now there's a thought, Mr Grant," he replied, giving his great rumbling laugh. "It occurred to me, Sir, that as we've come out here a'rescuing folk, we'd all look mighty foolish if we had to be rescued ourselves!"

Having satisfied myself that we had done all we could, we returned to the *Norseman* and were hoisted aboard. The surgeon was already busy with the survivors that *Octavius* had rescued, and from the condition of some of the men we had pulled from the water I doubted whether they would last the night. Towards evening word was passed around the fleet that Lord Nelson was dead, having been mortally wounded by a marksman from the rigging of an enemy ship. Many a hardened seaman was reduced to tears by the news, for the Admiral was much loved. I felt a great sense of loss, too, for it had long been my ambition to serve under him and I had only done so for a week or two, during which I had seen him but once, and that at a distance.

That night a fearful gale sprang up. It was not quite as bad as the one we had narrowly survived in the Caribbean, but it was bad enough. It lasted throughout the following day, and on into the next. Some of the survivors we had aboard said that the experience was worse than the battle. It was a severe test of seamanship, for we took in tow one of the dismasted prizes for a while until forced to cut her loose or perish ourselves.

During this period some of the more badly damaged prizes sank, while others were driven ashore and wrecked. In some cases our small prize crews were forced to release the original French or Spanish crews to help man the pumps and keep their ships afloat. Outnumbered by their prisoners as they were, they became prisoners in their turn and were taken into Cadiz. On 23rd October the enemy, hoping to recover yet more prizes, made a sortie from Cadiz, retaking two of them yet losing three of their number who were driven ashore and wrecked by the storm. Four days later Admiral Collingwood sent in a boat under flag of truce offering to return the French and Spanish wounded in return for the captured prize crews. The offer was gratefully accepted. Because of the storm, we only managed to bring four prizes into Gibraltar.

A few days later we were sent home with a number of senior French and Spanish officers aboard, awaiting exchange. It was the custom that officer prisoners-of-war could be exchanged for those of equal rank in the enemy's possession, or released if they gave a parole not to fight again during the war. There being no cabin space for them, our prisoners were forced to sling hammocks like the rest of us, at which they grumbled mightily, to our great amusement.

On 1st December 1805 I passed the Examination for Lieutenant, as indeed did all of *Norseman*'s midshipmen. The Examining Board, consisting of three Captains, was much interested to learn that we had been present at Trafalgar and questioned us about the battle. After looking through our certificates of service and logs they asked us a series of questions on navigation and seamanship, none of which we found difficult, so thorough had been our training. We returned to the ship elated and were summoned with the other officers to Captain Montague's cabin, where we were congratulated, wished well and plied with champagne. In a more sombre tone the Captain said that he, and the rest of the officers, would be joining us on half pay while we awaited appointments to other ships, as he had just received word that *Norseman* was to be decommissioned and her crew paid off. This was received sadly, for while it gave us a chance to visit our homes, we had become used to each other and it meant many goodbyes.

A week later, feeling a little self-conscious in my new Lieutenant's uniform, I collected my outstanding pay and prize money from my agent. I came across Armstrong in the street and asked him what the future held for him.

"Well, Mr Grant, just now I'm making my way to the coach office," he replied. "You see, Sir, it won't be long afore the word is passed that Joel Armstrong is back, and then there'll be those who'll want to try their luck in a fight with me. That's how my troubles started, so I'd like to get as far away from here as I can and maybe make a fresh start up north somewhere, where I'm less well known."

"That's a wise decision," I replied. "I'm leaving for Liverpool shortly, so why don't you join me? My father is a merchant there and he can always find work for a strong honest man."

"Well, Sir, that's handsome of you, Mr Grant," he said after a moment's thought. "You'll remember I once said I'd no wish to be beholden to any man. Well, over the past few years you and I have done each other a good turn or two and seen a good bit o' the world together, so I reckon that between us it's different. I'll avail myself of your kind offer, Sir, for which I'm most grateful."

I arrived home shortly before Christmas. My parents did not recognize me at first, expecting to see the boy they had sent to sea and finding him a man who was now taller than his father. I already knew from letters received that I had become an uncle several times over, and for the first time I met my nieces and nephews, the oldest of whom is five. Our neighbours were greatly impressed that I was at Trafalgar, although I assured them my part in the battle was very small. Nevertheless, I was forced to tell them the tale over and over again, as well as the story of my other adventures, until they came to regard me as some sort of hero, which I certainly was not. I experienced no difficulty in persuading Father to take on Armstrong, for whom we found decent clean lodgings near the docks.

With the coming of the New Year, I found myself beginning to miss the comradeship of the *Norseman* and all the many aspects of life at sea. I was also struck by the depressing thought that now that the French and Spanish have been defeated, I may have to wait for months, or even years, for another ship. However, on

22nd January, the post brought two items of good news. The first was that Parliament had awarded £300,000 to those present at Trafalgar. My share as a Midshipman at the time was £37. The second was a letter from Captain Montague:

James Grant, Esq, RN
My Dear James,
You will, I am sure, be pleased to learn that I have been given command of a 74, presently building at Chatham, and am in a position to offer you the appointment of her Fourth Lieutenant, should you be interested. To be sure, there will be fewer adventures aboard a ship-of-the-line than we had aboard the old Norseman, *but it will be a valued asset to your career, which has already shown much promise. Your early reply, hopefully containing your acceptance, would oblige me greatly.*

Please convey my regards to your family, which I am given to understand has grown considerably.

Your friend,
Charles Montague

I was walking to the Post Office with my acceptance when I decided to continue to Salthouse Dock, where

Armstrong could usually be found trundling bags and bales on his trolley. The thought occurred that he might be interested in joining me, and I was confident that Captain Montague would be happy to take aboard an experienced Gunner's Mate.

Glossary

Aft – towards the back or stern of a ship.

Aloft – any space above deck level.

Amidships – in the central part of the ship.

"Avast" – "stop".

Boatswain – officer responsible for the sails and rigging of a ship. Pronounced Bo'sun.

Braces – ropes fastened to the yardarms, enabling the yards to be moved so as to take advantage of the wind.

Brig – a two-masted, square-rigged vessel with topgallants on both masts .

Broadside – all the guns a ship could mount on one side or another; also refers to the firing of these guns.

Cable – a thick, heavy rope used in conjunction with an anchor.

Capstan – a rotating drum mounted vertically on the upper deck of a ship. Long bars, each manned by several men, could be inserted into the drum and pushed round, the power developed being used to raise the anchor. A large ship required over 90 men to man the bars.

Careen – to scrape the accumulated weeds and barnacles from ship's bottom after a long period at sea.

Cutting out – boarding and capturing an enemy ship in its own harbour, then taking it to sea.

Ensign – a national naval flag.

Fathom – a nautical measurement equalling six feet.

Fore – towards the front or bow of a ship.

Fore-and-aft rigged ship – a ship with the principal sails attached to the rear of the masts.

Frigate – respectably armed and capable of up to 14 knots, the most versatile warship of the era. It was often given an independent role such as convoy escort or commerce raider – patrolling and scouting for the battle fleet.

Gaff – a spar projecting backwards and upwards from the mizzen mast (see diagram, page 156).

Gig – the smallest of a ship's boats, usually reserved for the captain.

Gunner – officer responsible for the maintenance of the ship's guns and equipment, as well as the welfare and discipline of the Midshipmen.

Halliard – a rope for raising or lowering a ship's sail or flag.

"Handsomely" – "slowly".

143

"Heave-to" – to set one or more sails aback so as to bring the ship to a standstill.

Hull – the frame or body of a ship.

Knot – a measurement of speed; one knot equals one nautical mile (1.14 land miles) per hour.

Larboard – an alternative name for port (see below).

"Lay" – "go". A seaman ordered to "lay aft" would report to the senior officer on the Quarterdeck.

Leeward – to be furthest away from the direction in which the wind is blowing (pronounced loo'ard).

Letters of Marque – the official licence granted to a privateer to prey upon the King's enemies. In the United Kingdom they could be obtained for a modest fee at the Post Office. A privateer lacking these documents was treated as a pirate.

Orlop – the lowest deck in the ship, containing the junior officers' quarters. In action, being the safest place aboard, it was where the surgeon erected his operating table.

Overhaul – overtake.

Port – the left-hand side of a ship when facing forward.

Prize money – earned by the capture or destruction of enemy ships. The prize money awarded for Trafalgar was divided as follows: Captain, £3,362; Lieutenants and Masters, £226; Senior Warrant Officers, £153;

Midshipmen and Junior Warrant Officers, £37; Ordinary Seamen, £6.10.0d.

Rake – in gunnery, to sweep the entire length of a ship with shot.

Schooner – usually a small, fast fore-and-aft rigged ship, sometimes carrying topsails.

Sea-lawyer – a troublesome sailor who thinks he knows more about the regulations than his officers.

Ship-of-the-Line – sometimes called a Line-of-Battle ship. The principal fighting units of every navy, classified by the number of guns carried, which varied between 50 and 120, sited on two or three gun-decks. The most common was the 74. Hulls were constructed from thickened timber to keep out the enemy's shot.

Sloop – general term for a small warship mounting less than twenty guns.

Splice – to join the ends of different ropes together by inter-weaving their strands.

Square-rigged ship – a ship with the principal sails carried squarely across the masts, as opposed to a fore-and-aft rigged ship (see diagram, page 156).

Starboard – the right-hand side of a ship when facing forward.

Studding sail booms – extensions to a yard on which it

was possible to hoist additional sails.

Suit of sails – a complete set of sails.

Tackle – a device of pulleys (called blocks) and ropes for raising or securing heavy objects, or controlling the movement of guns, sails and yards.

Tender – a small boat which carries stores or passengers to or from a larger boat.

Waist – the central section of a ship, between and below the forecastle and the quarterdeck (see diagram, page 156).

Watch – a period of duty.

Windward – closest to the direction from which the wind is blowing.

Historical Note

In 1789 the French people rebelled against an unjust and corrupt system of government. It had taxed the ordinary people to the point of starvation yet allowed large sections of the wealthy to go untaxed. The principles upon which the French Revolution was based were Liberty, Equality and Brotherhood for all men, but the radical and violent methods employed by the revolutionaries so alarmed the monarchies of Europe that they attempted to crush the revolution by force, lest it spread to their own countries and destroy the established social order. In 1792 King Louis XVI of France and his Queen, Marie Antoinette, made an unsuccessful attempt to flee the country. They were tried for treason and executed the following year. In disgust, the United Kingdom expelled the French ambassador. France responded by declaring war. With one short break, the wars that ensued were to last for 22 years.

The French Revolutionary Wars and the Napoleonic Wars that followed presented a serious danger of invasion as well as a threat to the business of British merchants and shipowners. The French never succeeded in winning command of the sea and were therefore unable to mount a major invasion, although unsuccessful landings were made in Ireland and Wales. The Royal Navy's tasks during the war included preventing the Spanish or Dutch fleets combining with the French (which would give the enemy superiority) imposing a blockade on the French coast, and safeguarding British trade. The French strategy at sea was to prey upon British commerce, using privateers. These were particularly active in the Caribbean, where the islands of the West Indies were of immense economic importance to the United Kingdom and where the French also owned land. At this time, frigates such as this story's HMS *Norseman* were widely employed in the protection of British commerce, as well as acting as the eyes of the fleet by keeping watch on French activities.

One of the French Revolution's most ardent and able supporters was a young Corsican officer named Napoleon Bonaparte. His actions in defence of the Revolution led to his rapid promotion and as commander of the French Army of Italy he defeated the Austrians time after time. It was, however, fully appreciated by the new political masters of France that General Bonaparte was ambitious and therefore dangerous. In 1798, less than two years before James joined HMS *Norseman*, Bonaparte was allowed to lead an expedition to Egypt because this would conveniently keep him away from the corridors of power in Paris. On 1 August of that year, Admiral Horatio Nelson destroyed the French Mediterranean Fleet at the Battle of the Nile, and in so doing left Bonaparte marooned in Egypt for a while. Bonaparte, however, managed to escape to France and, having been elected First Consul, inflicted a crushing defeat on Austria, Great Britain's principal ally in Europe, at the Battle of Marengo in 1800. This, with the Army's support, set him on the road that would eventually see him crowned as Napoleon, Emperor of the French, on 2 December 1804.

Napoleon used the short Peace of Amiens to consolidate his hold on power and during this period sent his brother-in-law, General Victor Leclerc, to crush the slave rebellion in the French-owned Saint Domingue, known today as Haiti. This had broken out in 1791 when the slaves, not unreasonably, thought that the principles of the French Revolution applied to them, too, and a savage civil war had followed. Leclerc died from Yellow Fever on 2 November 1802. Toussaint L'Ouverture, the slave leader, whom he had treacherously captured, was imprisoned in a French castle, where he starved to death the following year. When the French withdrew their troops from Saint Domingue, Toussaint's successor, Jean Jacques Dessalines, ordered the massacre of every white remaining on the island. During this period and following the resumption of hostilities, the fictional HMS *Norseman*'s adventures in the Caribbean mirror those of many British warships serving on the West Indies station.

By 1805, Napoleon had decided that Great Britain was his most tenacious enemy. Aware that he could not launch an invasion of England until the Royal Navy's Channel Fleet was neutralized, he devised an ambitious but impractical plan. A French fleet under Vice Admiral Pierre Villeneuve broke out of Toulon and, picking up Spanish warships off Cadiz, sailed across the Atlantic to the Caribbean, where it reinforced the French garrisons in the West Indies. Villeneuve's orders now required him to prey upon British possessions in the area, then re-cross the Atlantic and break the British blockade of Brest and Ferrol, allowing the French and Spanish squadrons within to join him. This, it was calculated, would give him no less than 40 ships-of-the-line, enough to hold off the Channel Fleet while the French Grand Army was transported in safety to England. In the event, Villeneuve only attacked one small British island, then, having learned that Nelson was pursuing him, he decided to return to Europe rather than risk a battle with his semi-trained crews.

On 21 October 1805, Nelson finally succeeded in bringing Villeneuve to battle off Cape Trafalgar and utterly destroyed his fleet. Franco-Spanish casualties have been estimated at 8,000 killed and wounded and 20,000 prisoners. British losses totalled 437 killed and 1,242 wounded. Four of the enemy ships which escaped from the battle were captured during an engagement on 4th November. Admiral Villeneuve was sent back to France in 1806 but met a violent end in a hotel room only days after his return. Officially, he committed suicide, but the presence of five stab wounds suggests that Napoleon may have ordered his death.

After Trafalgar, Napoleon never again sought to challenge the Royal Navy at sea. Instead, he engaged in a series of wars on land, defeating the Austrians, Prussians and Russians between 1805 and 1809, creating kingdoms for his brothers and favourites from conquered territory. The Spaniards, however, refused to accept his brother Joseph as their king and rebelled. As a result, Great Britain despatched troops to assist Spain and Portugal, so beginning the Peninsula War, which lasted from 1807 until 1814 and ended with the French being finally ejected from Spain.

Napoleon finally overreached himself by invading Russia in 1812, a disastrous campaign from which only a fraction of his Grand Army returned. All the major European powers then converged on France, which no longer possessed the resources to resist an invasion. In 1814 Napoleon abdicated and was exiled to the island of Elba, off the Italian coast. The following year he escaped and raised fresh armies, only to be defeated by an Allied army led by the Duke of Wellington at the Battle of Waterloo. He abdicated for the second time and was exiled to St Helena in the south Atlantic, where he died in 1821.

Trafalgar ensured that the Royal Navy remained the dominant power on the world's oceans until well into the next century. Waterloo resulted in 40 years of uninterrupted peace for the nations of Europe.

The Slave Trade

Although the slave trade was abolished in the UK in 1807, slavery itself did not become illegal in British lands until 30 years later. And it took another 30 years, and a Civil War, before it was formally ended in the United States.

Even at the height of the trade, slaves were never shipped directly to England but, as James narrates, a few English-speaking second- or third-generation slaves were imported from the West Indies to serve in military bands or as domestic servants.

Picture acknowledgements

P156   Diagram of sailing ship, Maltings Partnership

P157   Map of the Caribbean in the early nineteenth century, András Bereznay

P158   Trafalgar battle plan, András Bereznay

P159 (top)   Midshipman Blockhead putting on his uniform..., George Cruikshank, © National Maritime Museum, London

P159 (bottom) Mr B finding things..., © National Maritime Museum, London

Timeline

1789 French Revolution begins on 17 June.

1791–1801 Slave rebellion and civil war in the French colony of Saint Domingue (Haiti).

21 January 1793 Execution of King Louis XVI of France. In protest, the British government expels the French ambassador. France, already at war with Austria and Prussia, declares war on Great Britain.

2 March 1796 Bonaparte appointed commander of the Army of Italy, subsequently winning numerous victories against the Austrians.

8 October 1796 Spain declares war on Great Britain.

16 April – 13 June 1797 Mutinies in the Channel and North Sea Fleets at Spithead and The Nore secure better conditions of service for seamen in the Royal Navy.

11 October 1797 Admiral Duncan defeats the Dutch fleet at Camperdown, off the Texel.

19 May 1798 Bonaparte sails for Egypt.

1 August 1798 Admiral Nelson destroys the French fleet at the Battle of the Nile.

23 August 1799 Bonaparte escapes to France.

14 December 1799 Bonaparte appointed First Consul.

14 June 1800 Bonaparte inflicts crushing defeat on the Austrians at Marengo.

1 October 1801 Great Britain and France sign the preliminaries of Peace of Amiens.

14 December French expedition sails to crush slave rebellion in Saint Domingue.

2 August 1802 Bonaparte proclaimed First Consul for life.

16 May 1803 Great Britain declares war on France.

15 June 1803 French Grand Army establishes a camp at Boulogne in preparation for the invasion of England.

November 1803 Demoralized and ravaged by disease, the French evacuate Saint Domingue. The remaining white population is massacred.

18 May 1804 Bonaparte proclaimed as Napoleon, Emperor of the French.

December 1804 Spain declares war on Great Britain.

21 October 1805 Franco-Spanish Combined Fleet destroyed by Admiral Nelson at the Battle of Trafalgar. British supremacy at sea remains virtually unchallenged for the rest of the war.

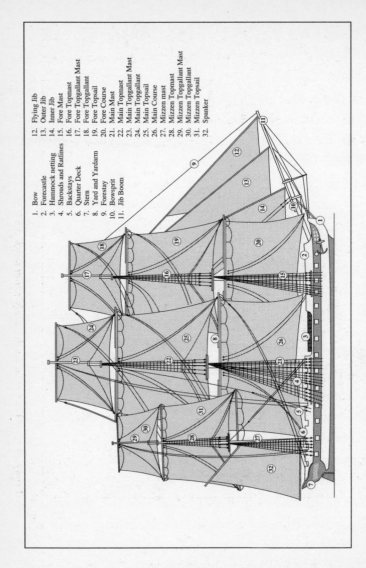

1. Bow
2. Forecastle
3. Hammock netting
4. Shrouds and Ratlines
5. Backstays
6. Quarter Deck
7. Stern
8. Yard and Yardarm
9. Forestay
10. Bowsprit
11. Jib Boom
12. Flying Jib
13. Outer Jib
14. Inner Jib
15. Fore Mast
16. Fore Topmast
17. Fore Topgallant Mast
18. Fore Topgallant
19. Fore Topsail
20. Fore Course
21. Main Mast
22. Main Topmast
23. Main Topgallant Mast
24. Main Topgallant
25. Main Topsail
26. Main Course
27. Mizzen mast
28. Mizzen Topmast
29. Mizzen Topgallant Mast
30. Mizzen Topgallant
31. Mizzen Topsail
32. Spanker

Sailplan and rig of a typical frigate – a square-rigged ship.

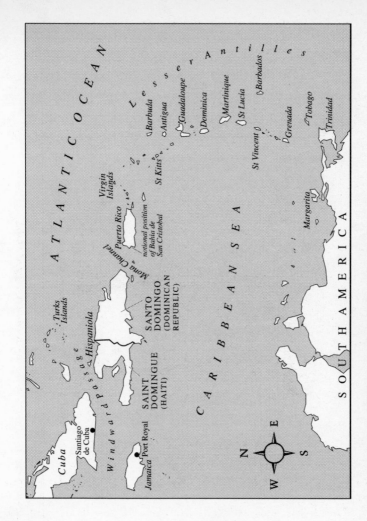

A map of the Caribbean in the early nineteenth century.

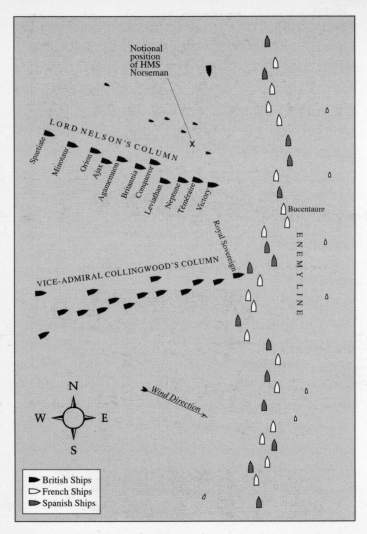

Notional position of HMS Norseman

LORD NELSON'S COLUMN

Spartiate
Minotaur
Orion
Ajax
Agamemnon
Britannia
Conqueror
Leviathan
Neptune
Temeraire
Victory

X

Bucentaure

ENEMY LINE

Royal Sovereign

VICE-ADMIRAL COLLINGWOOD'S COLUMN

N
W · E
S

Wind Direction

► British Ships
▷ French Ships
◪ Spanish Ships

A plan of the Battle of Trafalgar.

A young naval officer being fitted for his uniform.

A scene of life below the deck on board ship.

159

Also in the series:

CIVIL WAR

The Story of Thomas Adamson
England 1643-1650

BATTLE of
BRITAIN

The Story of Harry Woods
England 1939-1941

THE
TRENCHES

The Story of Billy Stevens
The Western Front 1914-1918